3-24-15

WHISPERING
WINDS REMEMBER

*"May the memories of your past be as soft and gentle
as the whispering winds reminding you of them."*

WHISPERING WINDS REMEMBER

DONALD L. ENSENBACH

TATE PUBLISHING
AND ENTERPRISES, LLC

Published by Tate Publishing & Enterprises, LLC
127 E. Trade Center Terrace | Mustang, Oklahoma 73064 USA
1.888.361.9473 | www.tatepublishing.com

Tate Publishing is committed to excellence in the publishing industry. The company reflects the philosophy established by the founders, based on Psalm 68:11,
"The Lord gave the word and great was the company of those who published it."

Published in the United States of America

ISBN: 978-1-63122-458-4
Fiction / Historical
14.10.07

The locations are, in the order of mention in the book:

Besh ba Lakado (Place by the Lake)—Tonto National Monument, Roosevelt, AZ.

Besh ba Gowah (Place of Metal)—Besh ba Gowah Archaeological Park, Globe, AZ.

Gila Village (next to the Salt River)—Pueblo Grande Museum, Phoenix, AZ.

Green Stone Village—Village of Peridot, AZ. (Indian village in Southeastern AZ)

Long River Village—Gila Cliff Dwellings National Monument, New Mexico

Large House Village—Casa Grande National Monument, Coolidge, AZ

Canyon of Walnut Trees—Walnut Canyon National Monument, Flagstaff, AZ

Village of Irapu—City of Tlaxcala, Mexico-mentioned, not visited in this book

LIST OF CHARACTERS

Little Star—Daughter of Kokopelli & White Moon

Gray Eagle—Deceased mate of Little Star & son of Straight Arrow

White Bear and Flying Eagle—Twin sons of Gray Eagle and Little Star

Brown Fox—Traveling trader partner of Little Star

Red Wolf—Shaman brother of Little Star

Yellow Moon & Full Moon—Mate and daughter of ShamanRed Wolf

Chief Koko-Who-Travels— Chief of Besh ba Gowah

Gray Fawn & Eagle Wing—Mate of chief Koko-Who-Travels & son

Black Coyote—Chief of village of Large House

Pretty Sky—Escaped harvester of crops for Village of Large House

Brave Beaver & Long Knife— mate and brother of Pretty Sky

Blue Nose—friend of Brave Beaver and Long Knife

Brave Hawk & Green Stalk— leaders of the hunters & gatherers at Besh ba Gowah

Blue Stone & Bright Sun—Teacher & shaman student at Besh ba Gowah

Long Bow and Little Mouse—Father & Mother of Brown Fox

Chief Two Owls and Singing Water—Chief and mate at LongRiver and Father and Mother of Yellow Moon

Chief Big Bear—Chief of the village of Green Stone

Brown Bear—Grandson of Big Bear of Green Stone

Red Skies—Widowed mother of Brown Bear

Gray Cougar—Shaman of the village of Green Stone

Kopel—Traveling trader & son of Peltar, friend of Kokopelli from Irapu

ACKNOWLEDGEMENTS

I must thank many people who have helped me in researching, getting me started writing these historical novels, and backing me with love, understanding, and the corrections I need to keep going on this effort. My wife of 54+ years, Opal, has been my biggest help. She is the reason I can afford to do these things that I enjoy, as she watches the checkbook, does my driving to the faraway places I appear and keeps me going in the right direction. Our three children, five grandchildren, and fifteen great-grandchildren are special, although we don't get to see them very often.

My editor, Keith Ougden, who winters in Mesa and summers on the island of Cyprus, is an invaluable friend and chief correction officer. I can't begin to tell you of the hours he spends reading and correcting the many errors I make, suggesting revisions of sentences and words that better tell the story. He, and his wife Virginia, are certainly wonderful friends and neighbors.

The artist for the covers of my books is Jay Nixon. I am very impressed by him as I call him, tell him my ideas for the cover, and he goes about painting them just as I describe them. Since all of my stories are legends and myths, I asked him to use black figures to represent the "shadows of the past," not the faces of real people, birds and animals.

I also get much help getting my computer to do what I want from Tom Baker, Opal's and my invaluable neighbor, a true guru.

As for the many other people who have been instrumental in helping me market the books I have written, I must thank the customer relations managers at the Barnes & Noble bookstores, the Arizona Hastings Entertainment stores, and the many smaller bookstores around the country that agree to allow me to appear at their locations. Steve at the Book Vault in Mesa, Shereen at the Book Boutique in Henderson, NV, Elizabeth at All In Books in West Bend, WI, the senior centers, churches, schools, and retirement parks holding Arts and Craft shows or Country Stores have been so important to me. Thank you all for your help and acceptance.

—Donald L. Ensenbach

CHAPTER 1

The trail leading downward from the overlook they had reached lay before them as Brown Fox, Little Star, White Bear, the female wolf and its two cubs made their way carefully along the top of the hill. The eerie sound of a wolf howl carried on the winds surrounding the travelers, and sent shivers down the spine of Little Star. She knew that it was the howl of her wolf, the male wolf that she had helped those many summers ago. She removed a stone from between the claws of its right forepaw before allowing it to lead her to this overlook during the middle of the night. From here, she had seen for the first time the beautiful blue waters of the lake bathed in the bright moon and starlight, and the valley below that offered the land to be the location of Besh ba Lakado, their new village site. She remembered how it had become necessary for the people of Gila, her village, to find a new location. Her spirit father, Kokopelli, had seen this exact view during an earlier dream catcher and had described it to the villagers. Little Star had been included in a group to search for this place. She had led the group to this very spot on the morning after the wolf showed her the way.

She remembered that it had been the same male wolf that had accompanied her mate, Gray Eagle, on his fateful quest to visit the ledge on the mountain beyond the lake toward the sunrise direction. It had been a cougar that had attacked from above, knocking Gray Eagle to the ground, causing him to be paralyzed and defenseless while the cougar savagely killed him. His remains had been found by a group of hunters from the village led by his father, Straight Arrow. The wolf had apparently gone hunting in another direction before the attack, and was snared by a trap from which it could not escape, and it too died.

Little Star's mind filled with memories as they continued walking down toward the open area where Brown Fox, White Bear and she would spend the night, hoping for a restful sleep. It had been there she had first heard the sound of crying that wakened her, and after following the sound into the woods, had found the injured wolf. It was also the place at which five coyotes had attempted to attack Little Star, Gray Eagle, Brown Fox, and her twin sons on their way to Besh ba Lakado just two fall seasons before. The female wolf which was now pulling the travois that was carrying their trading goods had protected them from the attacking coyotes, killing their leader and putting the others to flight, just before the male wolf joined the travelers. Yes, this place was fondly remembered by Little Star.

Little Star, along with her mother, White Moon, Kokopelli, their family and friends had made the move from the Gila village alongside the Salt River to what was now the village of Besh ba Lakado (Place by the Lake). She had been five summers old at that time, and her best friend and playmate, Gray Eagle, had later become her mate. But that seemed so long ago, almost as if in an earlier life. Now she had to find a new life for herself, her son White Bear, with Brown Fox as her trading partner. The trained birds that now flew between her and Brown Fox, and the wolves that pulled the travois, had become valued as close as family members.

Now it was time to prepare the campsite for the night. Carefully, Brown Fox and Little Star surrounded the camp with a protective circle of brush around the campfire, an area for the travois with the trading goods still attached, a space for the woven sleeping mats to be spread, and a rock to which the wolves were tethered not too tightly. Actually, the clearing was a small fortress-like area that would protect the group from outside prowlers, and would help keep the wolves from wandering away during the night without being noticed.

After warming up a sparse meal of traveling food, eating, cleaning up and burying the scraps, the group settled down for a night's sleep. The strenuous steep climb from Besh ba Lakado had tired the group, and they decided to get an early start on their dream catchers. The sounds of the softly blowing winds through the forested mountains around them did not disturb them as they were not used to the exercise of hiking up and over the trail.

Brown Fox fell asleep and dreamed about the adventure he was resuming, traveling from village to village, meeting old and new friends, trading goods with many villagers, visiting new places, and above all, returning to his home of Long River to see his mother and father. Before arriving there, however, they would stop at the village of Besh ba Gowah to see if Yellow Moon, his first love, and Red Wolf her mate, had stayed there or left to rejoin her family in the village of Long River.

Little Star had drifted off to a fitful sleep, which was interspersed with memories of the times she had spent sleeping at this level space perched along the backside of the Thunder God's mountain. Two of the most important nights of her life were spent here, and a third was taking shape in her conscious mind as she dreamed.

She was being visited by the spirit world. First there was her mother White Moon, who laid her hand on Little Star's brow and whispered to her, "You have brought much happiness to your spirit father, Kokopelli, and me. We watch you from our home above, and approve of the way you have handled the issues you have faced during your young life. There will be more in your future, but hold fast to your ideals, and think and work through them as you have in the past." As the last word was whispered, the image of White Moon faded away, and was replaced by Gray Eagle. A small flame burned from his naked chest where his heart would be, and his eyes spoke silently of his love for her. As his image approached her, his whispers and the feel of his hot breath on her ear and neck made her shiver involuntarily. The sounds were like sweet music expressing his deep love for her and the assurance that he would be watching her from high above. His last words were "Watch for our son Flying Eagle to be seen by many people over the next many days and nights. The "Great One" has chosen our son to unite the people in great villages for their protection and the progress of the world." And then his image faded away. These appearances and messages were retained in Little Star's dream catcher, while a fearful one went through and was lost.

The following morning brought birds and animals to the river bank for their baths and drinks of the cold clear water even before the sunrise. The huge thirsting valley far below would appreciate this water, but it would take days of meandering through the many channels of the Salt River before it would emerge into the narrow ribbon leading westward through the lower center of the desert valley and past the old Gila village from which she had moved.

Little Star remembered the legend of how this river was named, as her spirit father, Kokopelli, the famous traveling trader, had told the story one cold night around the village campfire. He told of a village, much like the village of Gila from which they came, where the water and food supply was diminishing. They needed to find a new location for their village. They had packed up and left the old village site, walking toward the faraway mountains in hopes of finding a new home. Having walked all morning, the mate of the chief confessed that she had left a certain big basket that had been woven by the chief's mother back in the village next to the door of their hut. She knew that his mother had promised the god of the water plant from which she had taken the fronds, that she and her family would never mistreat, or abandon the basket. The chief asked their young daughter to go back and retrieve the basket. She and her little dog walked back to the old village site, picked up the basket and began walking back to the place where she had left the family. But, they were not there anymore, and it was getting dark. She spotted a cave in a little hill nearby, and carefully climbed inside. It was dark and scary, and she let out a sniffle. Sitting down with her back against the wall, she allowed her little dog to sit on her lap. She heard a frightening noise, and gave out a short scream. She was terrified of the dark and strange noises. Then, she heard the sound of her father's voice saying, "Little Indian girls do not cry." That was not much help to her though, and she cried with the tears pearling on her hands and falling onto the sand in front of her. Those tears spilled through the sands, entering the great river that flowed beneath the cave, turning it slightly salty. Thereafter, it was called the Salt River.

As the pleasant memory of Kokopelli's story about the origin of the Salt River came to an end, Little Star realized that she was next to the water that furnished that river its flow. The water up here was clear and cool, so the rabbit-skin bags were filled, slung around the necks of Brown Fox and Little Star and taken over to the encircled area of the camp in which they had slept. White Bear was on his hands and knees, crawling around trying to catch the female cub wolf, but it had played the game before and stayed just far enough in front to keep the boy's interest, but not allow the clutching of its leg or tail. Brown Fox fastened the travois to the female wolf's sides. Little Star picked up White Bear and set him in the cradle-board, which had become more of a backward-facing chair, and Brown Fox helped strap it to Little Star's back. Then, they scattered the branches that had encircled their camp before setting off on their downward journey between the mountainside and the water spilling down the river from above.

Little Star and Brown Fox had trained birds to fly between them as she and Gray Eagle had trained their birds before. It was a perfect time to allow the newly trained birds to fly around them as they carefully descended the trail from the top toward the front face of the Thunder God's mountain.

The travel down was extremely dangerous as the female wolf had to both pull and brake the travois as it moved over and around rocks, got stuck in small depressions and got caught on roots sticking out of the ground. Brown Fox had to remain beside the wolf, encouraging it to zigzag around the trouble spots, while Little Star was very careful to avoid rocks and vegetation that might make her fall or lose her balance. This was far different than the last time she had come down this pathway with Gray Eagle at her side.

They stopped another time to sleep before reaching the level area in front of the Thunder God's mountain. This was not as protected from the wind, as it was farther from the mountainside and the trees were not as dense as at the first stopping place. They fashioned a circle of branches and packs around their sleeping mats, travois, and the shallow fire pit that had been built in the center of the campsite. They would have some fried rabbit strip and a soup of soft leaves Little Star had picked as they passed through an area of some young trees that had branches that were low enough for her to reach. It was a bit early in the spring for the red and blueberries to be picked and eaten, but she was sure that they would find some of those on the warmer, level areas of the desert after making the turn toward the sunrise direction they would be reaching the next day or two. The birds were in the cages and the wolves were tethered to a root from a nearby tree stump. After the food had been eaten, the young travelers readied the camp to bed down. Just then, a noisy hawk swooped down and picked up a small piece of rabbit that had fallen to the ground in front of White Bear. Little Star remembered the eagle picking up her son, Flying Eagle, in a similar manner, and screamed as she saw the bird dive down toward White Bear. She reached out, pulling White Bear toward her and holding him close to her heaving breast. She continued to scream until the hawk was out of sight, carrying away the single small piece of food it seemed to be after. Brown Fox had been feeding the birds and wolves, and rushed over to comfort Little Star, but it took some time for her to calm herself.

Sleep did not come easily to Little Star that night. She lay on her side, watching White Bear while he slept peacefully, she reliving the terrible moments when the eagle had swooped down, picked up Flying Eagle, and carried him off over the lake and beyond the mountains. Although the hawk was not the size of the eagle, the noise and the invasion it had made against their camp, toward her son, made her shake uncontrollably several times as she tried to rest. How many times must she relive those terrible, painful moments? Finally, she fell into a fitful sleep, but her dream catchers were not the type she would remember in the morning.

The next morning, after the water bags were filled and brought back to the campsite, a cool bath in the water of the river across the clearing was enjoyed by Brown Fox and Little Star, but the squealing complaints of White Bear let them know cool baths were not to his liking. After drying and dressing themselves, and then White Bear, a quick morning meal was eaten, consisting of bird eggs that had been taken from a hidden nest by the riverbank. Then it was time to hitch up the travois to the female wolf. This was a very important day for the traveling traders. They would be using the female wolf in the morning and hitch up the younger wolves, one at a time, to pull the travois during the afternoon. The female wolf would lead the younger ones, flanked by Brown Fox on one side and Little Star on the other until the switch was made. That occurred as they stopped in front of the Thunder God's mountain, right under the huge bow-like figure of the ship far above. From where they stopped, they could have seen the statues of the non-believers whom the "Great One" had turned to stone during the great flood, had they looked up. But, Little Star chose not to look, and did not mention the location to Brown Fox, so they passed by that fateful location without acknowledging its presence.

As they loosened the straps from around the back and shoulders of the female wolf, it looked back at Brown Fox, in confusion. It had not been released during the middle of the day unless they were stopping to make camp. When the young female wolf sidled over near its mother, Brown Fox rubbed its side closest to him, and it backed up closer to him. He placed the straps around its neck, across its chest, between its legs, around the shoulders and onto its back. After the straps had been secured, the young wolf looked around and started pulling the travois, just as its mother had done earlier. The mother wolf came over to the front of the young wolf licking its face as if to stop it until Brown Fox and Little Star had steadied the travois and positioned themselves at the sides of the young wolf. The mother wolf stepped aside and positioned itself next to Little Star as they began walking again toward their goal of the village of Besh ba Gowah. The front of the Thunder God's mountain and the gruesome rock statues at the sides of the bow of the ship high above were left behind as the travelers followed the path that had been taken by Gray Eagle and Little Star three early summers before. Each step she took reminded Little Star of the earlier trip, and she missed the companionship and the love Gray Eagle and she had shared. Now, she had a young man, Brown Fox, accompanying her and her son White Bear, along with the female wolf and its two young offspring. It was the same path, but two very different circumstances.

As the sun moved behind the travelers and their shadows were growing longer, the two young wolves exchanged places, with the young male wolf being hitched to the travois and the female that had been pulling the travois released to walk beside its mother. The young wolves had learned their jobs from their mother, and earned their rights to become part of the traveling group headed toward the village of Besh ba Gowah. It was a sense of pride that Little Star and Brown Fox felt when they saw how willingly the wolves took to helping with the transporting of the goods for trading. It allowed for searching and collecting of food along the pathway, the birds to be released to fly above and around them, and the freedom not to have to watch every step the wolves were taking. The happy sound of Little Star playing her flute led to the songs that Brown Fox would make up as they walked together, with White Bear sitting in his seat strapped to his mother's back. White Bear was happy to watch the trail behind, "oohing" and "ahhing" as the butterflies and even some of the hummingbirds flew around the bushes, cacti and small trees that grew alongside the trail. This was happiness of a different sort than when Little Star and Gray Eagle were starting out that first time winding their way around the Thunder God's mountain. Then, there had been wonder and excitement seeing the area that had been new to them, but now, Little Star had seen the path twice before, searching for the trail toward Besh ba Gowah and returning from there after the birth of the twin boys White Bear and Flying Eagle. Brown Fox had seen this trail before while traveling from Besh ba Gowah to Besh ba Lakado with Gray Eagle, Little Star, the two boys, and the female wolf. This was a comfortable feeling for all of them, knowing where the water, hills and shadows lay ahead of them. They were coming to the point at which the green trees at the bottom of the mountain indicated that the river held water. That would be the last place they could replenish their water bags before heading over the small group of hills and valleys leading up toward the area where Gray Eagle had seen the cougar at the stream near the bottom of the mountain. This, then, would be a perfect place to camp for the night.

The young male wolf was unharnessed from the travois by Brown Fox while Little Star removed the chair-cradleboard from her back, and lifted White Bear out, setting him on his stubby little feet. He danced around in a small circle before falling on his backside, laughing and giggling. He had fallen next to a rabbit burrow, and as he reached over with his left hand to right himself, he caught the furry neck of a curious rabbit that had stuck its neck out of the burrow, pinning the rabbit to the opposite side. White Bear had done his first successful hunting providing Little Star, Brown Fox and himself with meat for two evening meals. Little Star reached down and pulled the rabbit from its hole, broke its neck and laid it down next to where the small campfire would be started. She cut the rabbit's underside from neck to the tail, stripping the skin from the body. The meat was placed in a pan, would be heated after the fire was started, part would be eaten, while the rest was saved for the next day's evening meal. The skin was hung up to dry on a branch of a nearby cactus within the circle that had been built by Brown Fox. The circle consisted of a few branches from a dead tree fallen next to the river, tumbling weeds held in place by some large stones, and the loaded travois.

The pieces of flint carried by Little Star for the purpose of starting the campfire were brought out from her pouch she wore around her neck. She assembled the short, thin twigs in a small bowl-like hole and peeled the meat from the bones of the rabbit. A dish with a small amount of water would be used to cook the meat, and some of the water from the bags they had carried during the day would be used for that purpose. A few of the berries they had found along the trail would serve as a fitting end to the meal.

All the while this was going on White Bear was playing tag with the two young wolves, rolling around in the sand, getting very dusty in the process. The mother wolf sat resting on its haunches watching the three young friends playing. Its ears perked up as it heard the flapping wings of some large vultures looming overhead, watching where the bones of the rabbit were being discarded by Little Star. After starting the fire, placing the dish between the top of two rather large stones, Little Star turned away to take the bones outside the circle away from the river. She had not returned to the circle before the vultures swooped down for the feast they had been awaiting.

The meal was eaten and Brown Fox and Little Star cleaned up the area within the circle. Tethering the two young wolves to the cactus which held the rabbit skin out of their reach, and preparing the sleeping mats for themselves and White Bear, they lay down to sleep just as the moon and stars became the only light outside of the smoldering campfire. The crackling had subsided and the smoke had cleared as the travelers drifted off to their dream catchers.

Little Star's dream was visited by Gray Eagle. There he was, dressed in his finest rabbit-skin breechcloth, his bare chest shining as though in the mid-day sun, and a beautiful necklace of sparkling stones around his neck. His spirit approached her and spoke saying, "Little Star, my love, I am so very proud of what you are doing. You are doing exactly what we had planned on doing together. My spirit is with you as you travel onward toward the places and people we had visited before. The life you live will be honoring me in the things you do for others, as well as Brown Fox, White Bear and yourself. Keep in mind that not everything you seek will be as you have hoped, but changes occur for a reason, as the "Great One" allows. It is He that provides the good things people wish and pray for, but also brings reality back into everyone's lives and deaths. He has honored our youngest son, Flying Eagle, with the most important job for everyone who will ever live upon Mother Earth. Many people whom we have known have seen him since he left your breast. You, too, will see him sometime in the future. Be well, my love, and I will visit you in your dream catcher from time to time." His features faded away from her view although he never turned from facing her. A restful sleep was enjoyed by her as she was happy to feel Gray Eagle's presence enter her mind and heart, even for that short while.

Brown Fox had a different dream catcher. His was the realization that he now was the man responsible for the success or failure of the quest of Little Star, White Bear and himself to become the traveling traders he had dreamed so often of becoming. He began to go over the route from this place to the village of Besh ba Gowah, step-by-step, as he had followed Gray Eagle and Little Star the first time he had been on this pathway. He knew of the dangers of which Gray Eagle had warned him. The stream at which a cougar had been drinking, the roiling river below the canyon with the overhang that darkened the trail, and the passes that must be crossed before entering the village with the waterfall. It was not easy being responsible for others. He offered thanks to the "Great One" for the company and help of the female wolf and the two young wolves. They would offer some protection that might be needed along the way. He was not familiar with the ways of the wild animals, the wrath of the heat, winds and rain. His memory was his greatest help, next to the feeling of the guiding hands of the "Great One." Step-by-step he thought his way to the very welcoming entrance to Besh ba Gowah.

White Bear was happy to be with his mother, Little Star, and his friends, Brown Fox and the wolves. They had all acted very proud of him after he had snared the rabbit that late afternoon. He had been honored with the first bite of rabbit meat, and had a few extra berries as an extra treat. He had hopes of being allowed to walk alongside his mother or the wolves as they walked all day long. Well, maybe they would let him walk some of the way, and then be carried in his seat on his mother's back. He would watch the two birds that his mother and Brown Fox would release to fly around them for a period of time each day. He never had any bad thoughts the whole night through.

The morning was cool as the slight wind rose from behind them as they continued on their trek up the hills and through the valleys, onward toward the area of the stream at which they dreaded the sight of the cougar. Little Star longed for the assurance of Gray Eagle that the cougar would not be there when they grew closer, but of course, that was not to be. Brown Fox found a short stick about the length of his height from which he whittled a sharp point. This would not protect them from an attacking wild animal, but it was the best he could do for the moment. He hoped and prayed that the three wolves would be helpful in protecting his friends whom he felt responsible to and for.

The first pass came into view during the early afternoon, but it would be too late to make it to the top where they had met Kopel, the traveling trader from the village of Irapu, far to the hot winds direction. Deciding to camp in the middle of the valley rather than on the side of the hill, the camp was laid out in a short period of time, and the last of White Bear's rabbit meat was prepared and eaten. Again, White Bear had first bite, and there was cactus fruit eaten as an extra treat.

After the tired travelers bedded down, the female wolf left the camp on the prowl for food for its human friends and its own family. It returned a while later with a quail in its mouth, dropping it near the fire pit where the coals had already died out. It did not wake anyone, but stealthily, the wolf slipped out of camp again looking for more food for the group. Upon the second return it brought a small wild turkey, once more laying it next to the fire pit. It was not only a protector, but a provider for its family and companions.

The next morning's departure was delayed because of the preparation of the turkey and quail by de-feathering and cutting up the edible sections of each, and wrapping them inside a large rabbit skin pouch brought along for just this purpose. The large black vultures swooped in after the travelers left the bones and inedible parts of both behind. Climbing the hill toward the pass was done after the sun had been up for awhile, and the rays shone directly in the eyes of the climbers. The female wolf had been harnessed to the travois, and pulled it to the top of the pass, but was released in favor of the young male wolf, which seemed to be waiting for its chance to walk next to Brown Fox who had been leading the group up the hill.

After all the climbing, the level walking was easier on the legs of the entire group, but the young wolf clearly wanted to be the leader of the pack. White Bear had been set on his feet after reaching the level area, and was toddling along between Little Star and the young female wolf. He and the wolf had become close playmates. It was almost a game as White Bear would grab at the wolf's tail as it walked a little ahead of him, and then it would slow down and nip at White Bear's little behind causing him to laugh and giggle. Then it would trot up next to White Bear and the game would start over again.

By mid-afternoon, the pass had been reached and as they peered over the top it looked as though there were tracks that had approached from the hot wind direction and turned to follow the pathway they were headed. There was no indication as to whom it was that made the tracks, and nothing was within sight ahead of them. They would have to be extra cautious as they moved ahead, hoping that the people who made the tracks were friendly. Since there had been winds that picked up sand which filled in part of the footprints, they were not sure whether the prints were left by males or females. It appeared as though the length between the toes and heels of the next step were short, which could indicate any number of things from advanced age, a heavy burden, or weariness. It did not appear to indicate any hurried steps, but rather searching for a pathway that may lead to food or water. By looking off to the left and down a half-day's travel, they could see the glint of the stream at which the cougar had been spotted the first time that Gray Eagle and Little Star had walked this route. The green trees indicated that water still wove a course next to the mountain.

They camped just beyond the very top of the pass where the wind would blow over the top of the campsite, although it would not provide protection from the blowing dust that would settle upon them overnight. It was still early enough in the spring to be very cool at night, but it would warm up as the sun made its way through the normally blue skies during the days. There was very little with which to build a barrier around the small campsite, but the travois, cradleboard-chair seat and the wolves were stationed around in a circle to form the fence. Brown Fox took the young male wolf with him to search for a small straight branch to use as a sturdier spear, if needed, during the rest of the travel to Besh ba Gowah. Up to now there was no need for a weapon, but with the thought of the cougar near the stream and the people ahead of them on the trail, it was best to take no chances without some type of protection. Sleep came uneasily for the travelers this night, but the dream catchers provided both Brown Fox and Little Star assurance that the following day would bring them another day closer to Besh ba Gowah, Little Star's brother, Red Wolf and his mate, Yellow Moon, Brown Fox's friend. The question still remained as to whom did the footsteps represent, friend or foe?

The beautiful colored streaks of pink, purple, red and yellow broke above the few clouds drifting over the side of the mountain giving way to the brilliant sunlight cascading down upon them as the travelers remembered the good dreams caught in their dream catchers during the night. Yes, they were assured that this day would be a wonderful day in which they would find themselves another day closer to their friends in Besh ba Gowah. Brown Fox picked up the pace walking carefully down the trail from the pass, angling off toward the stream while carrying his spear. He was accompanied by the mother female wolf, with the young female wolf harnessed to the travois, White Bear in the cradleboard-chair seat attached to Little Star's back, and the young male wolf bringing up the rear. Every so often, the young male wolf would bolt to the front, only to be shooed back by Brown Fox. It was a bit slow in learning its part in the group of travelers.

As they followed the path to near the stream, they saw some vultures circling above a rock outcropping next to the trail. As they drew closer, Brown Fox saw a body sitting against the largest boulder. Cautiously, he approached, temporarily scaring the vultures away. Seeing that it was a woman who looked to be asleep, Little Star caught up to Brown Fox and approached the unconscious form. She was shocked when she recognized that it was Pretty Sky, the woman who was one of the harvesters of food grown at the village of Large House. Gray Eagle, Brown Fox and Little Star had met Pretty Sky as she worked in the fields of the village of Large House, and it was she who led them through the gates, past the armed guards, and in front of the big house occupied by the leader, Black Coyote. She was not asleep, but had collapsed and her breathing was very uneven. Brown Fox reached down for one of his filled water bags, opening it up slightly, and poured some out on his hand. He rubbed some onto her fevered forehead, and over her face. It was not cold, but it was wet, and her eyes opened to a small slit, and widened when she saw Little Star standing in front of her. Pretty Sky's throat was too parched to speak, but she looked at Little Star and then Brown Fox with eyes that spoke of her gratitude. She had expected to die there, next to the rocks, without any water or food. As a small amount of water was placed on her lips she opened her mouth and her tongue lolled out searching for more water. A little at a time was given to her, enough to moisten and loosen her vocal chords. She began to get her senses back and tried speaking, but the sounds were not understandable words.

Finally she explained, "I have run away from Black Coyote and his guards. Their insistence on us bringing them all of the food that we grew for ourselves and our children, and allowing us just enough to keep us alive and serving them, was more than I could take. I ran away when I was working in the fields, but that night one of the guards began following me. I saw him from the top of the hill behind us here, and I began running. I saw this pile of rocks and hoped to hide here without him finding me, but I grew too tired to run further, and here I lay down to die. I haven't seen him, so he may have passed by on the main trail, or left me for dead if he did see me."

Since the sun was beginning to settle over the hill behind them, and the fact that the water was only a short distance from where they were, Little Star suggested to Brown Fox, "We should make camp right next to this rock pile so that Pretty Sky can rest and eat the evening meal with us." A camp was laid out with room for the sleeping mats surrounded by the travois, some of the branches of a dead tree that had fallen over between the rocks and the stream, and a few of the staves from a dead Saguaro cactus. The travois had been unhitched from the young female wolf, and that wolf began to pace around the inside of the enclosed circle. A cold meal with the leftover dried turkey meat moistened with some fresh water and a few berries that had been growing on a bush next to the stream were enough to satisfy the hunger of the small group of humans, but the wolves left the camp to scrounge up what they could find.

As the moon became the main source of light, and the twinkling stars appeared far behind, the weary people bedded down for the night. Snores were loud and clear from Pretty Sky, a few giggles escaped from White Bear dreaming about the games he had been playing with the young wolves, while Brown Fox worried about the extra mouth to feed as they made their way toward Besh ba Gowah. Little Star dreamed about the danger to White Bear, Brown Fox and herself, that the discovery of Pretty Sky had brought upon them.

A noise off to the side of the circle that was nearest to the stream wakened both Brown Fox and Little Star. Brown Fox had laid the sharpened spear near his right thigh, where he could reach it if needed, and he grasped it stealthily as he felt, more than saw, a large figure stepping over the travois pack. Just then, three shadows lunged from the side, felling the figure to the ground as the wolves let out savage snarls as they bit into the offending figure's body. Screams of terror wakened Pretty Sky and White Bear, and White Bear began to cry. Brown Fox, Little Star and Pretty Sky all rose to see what was happening, but they looked down at three wolves attacking the hands, legs and body of an overpowered man lying on the ground with no way of defending himself. It was over in a few seconds, with the last breaths of the man squeezed through a broken face. The wolves pulled the broken body to the very far side of the encircled camp. They pushed aside the saguaro staves, pulling the remains of the man out of the camp and down toward what appeared to be a deep ravine. Something went thump back there, and the wolves returned to camp. They had done their duty and protected their adopted family, and their adopted family could not have been more grateful. The two female wolves lay down to sleep, but the young male wolf left the campsite, once more looking for food. It never seemed to tire out.

Upon wakening to a beautiful sunrise, Little Star and Pretty Sky took White Bear, accompanied by the three wolves, to the stream to fill the water bags and then wash in the cool water. Brown Fox had been up earlier, looking into the deep ravine where he saw the remains of the guard who had been following Pretty Sky. Next, he went to the stream looking for bird eggs for the morning meal, but finding none, picked more of the berries and brought them back to the camp. After the group returned with the water bags filled, they sat down for the morning meal of quail, and began preparing for the day's walk. This day would take them to the dark canyon corridor through which they would hurry. They would hear the sounds of the rushing water in the deep canyon below, opposite the walls that would lean over them while they rushed to return to the brilliant sunshine waiting for them on the other end. This was Little Star's least favorite part of the trip to Besh ba Gowah, but it would be worth it to see her brother, Red Wolf and his mate Yellow Moon, again.

As they approached the yawning opening to the dark canyon, two men emerged from it walking toward them and heartily chanting a song of praise to the "Great One." As they cleared the mouth of the opening, Pretty Sky began shouting and running toward the men. They saw her and began running toward her. It appeared to Brown Fox and Little Star to be three friends meeting, and hugging followed. As they approached the three, Pretty Sky separated from the two men, turned and said proudly, "Little Star and Brown Fox, I want you to meet my mate, Brave Beaver, and my brother, Long Knife. They left Large House when Black Coyote ordered the men to go and transport large logs to support another level to his big house. They were not born to be slaves, and told me of their wish to leave and live as free men. I am overjoyed to find and see them again. They will lead us into their new village of Besh ba Gowah."

CHAPTER 2

As they entered the village of Besh ba Gowah, shouts of recognition came from many areas that Brown Fox and Little Star remembered. From the sounds of the first shouts of welcome, chief Koko-Who-Travels came striding from his home. Holding out his arms in welcome, he said, "Ho ah, and welcome Little Star, sister to my mate, Gray Fawn! I see that Brown Fox is with you and you have a family of wolves with you, but where is Gray Eagle, your mate, and you have only one of your twin sons with you. Where are they?" Little Star answered, "Ho ah chief Koko-who-Travels! It is good to return to Besh ba Gowah and see many of the people with whom we have traded. Gray Eagle has walked the path to the happy hunting grounds, and our son, Flying Eagle was taken from me by a huge eagle. These are deep wounds that continue to affect me badly, and I wish to tell the stories once after a village evening meal, rather than many times. Would that be acceptable to you, chief Koko-Who-Travels?" He replied, "I understand your feelings and agree that once will be hard enough for you."

Just then, Gray Fawn, chief Koko-who-Travels' mate, came walking swiftly toward them. She was carrying a small child in her arms, and appeared to be overjoyed at the sight of her sister, Little Star. She greeted her with the traditional, "Ho ah sister Little Star. I am very happy to see you again. We have many things to talk about. I am sure you want to know that your brother Red Wolf and his mate Yellow Moon had a daughter named Full

Moon after Gray Eagle and you left our village. Then they left to return to Yellow Moon's home village of Long River. Upon their departure, the village accepted me as the shaman, and I pray to the "Great One" that I can become as good as Red Wolf was. Also, chief Koko-Who-Travels and I have a young son named Eagle Wing who was born during the late part of the stormy season. But, where is your mate, Gray Eagle and your second son? I don't see them with you."

Chief Koko-who-Travels broke in and mentioned that many things had happened to Little Star and her family during their absence from Besh ba Gowah, and because of the nature of the events, Little Star had asked to tell the stories once at a village evening meal, rather than recounting the events two or more times.

By this time, Brave Beaver, Pretty Sky, and her brother, Long Knife had also drawn a group of six men who encircled the three. The men began asking many questions of Pretty Sky. It appeared as though these men had escaped the clutches of Black Coyote and left the village of Large House when they were commanded to find and bring back large logs from faraway places to reinforce the upper stories of the big house. They all seemed to know Pretty Sky, and were interested in knowing of their families still remaining in the village of Large House. They began planning to ask that Pretty Sky speak during the evening meal in order to possibly form a group to travel to that village and bring their families to this village.

As Brown Fox and Little Star's group followed the chief and his mate through the village toward the special hut used by visitors to Besh ba Gowah, Little Star and Brown Fox were aware that the village had grown since their last visit. There were at least ten new huts built, with one being taller than the rest. Apparently, this was used by a lookout who might see all the way around the village, with four good-sized openings facing the primary directions. The flat roof with slightly elevated walls could offer a complete viewing platform during the hot summer heat, while the second story openings could be used during the cold and stormy seasons. The increase in huts meant an increase in residents, which would mean the trading should be better than before. They would hear the reasons for the growth at the evening meal, but were sure much of it had to do with the men arriving from the village of Large House.

Arriving at the hut they had used during their past visit to Besh ba Gowah, the wolf was unharnessed from the travois, but since it was the young female wolf which had not been among people other than the ones in Besh ba Lakado, a small leader rope of woven cotton was tied around its neck. Another was tied around the young male wolf's neck with both anchored to an exposed root of an agave cactus at the side of the hut. The adult female wolf had been in the village before, and the older children who had seen and played with it at that time came over to brush its sides and the fur above its eyes. It stood patiently as one after another took turns brushing and patting its body. It had not had this much attention since it had left Besh ba Lakado, and seemed to enjoy the touch of the youngsters' hands.

The travois was unloaded by Brown Fox and Little Star while White Bear was getting to play with some of the slightly older children from the village. He had to learn the important lesson of sharing when one of the playmates presented an animal toy figure to him, and then took it back. After a few squeals of irritation, a give-and-take form of acceptance was learned, and the laughing and giggling became normal activity. This was the first time that White Bear had been with children just a little older than he was, and he was enjoying every moment.

After the travois was unloaded and the contents stored inside the hut, the travois poles were stood against the outside back of the hut. Brown Fox took the remaining water bags to the side of the brook emptying them downstream from where they would refill them for their daily use in the mornings. It was really nice to be back at the village of Besh ba Gowah where he had last seen Yellow Moon, but now she had left with Red Wolf and gone back to Long River, her home village, and Brown Fox's home village as well. He was sure that Little Star would want to go from Besh ba Gowah directly to Long River so that she could see her brother, Red Wolf again. He began to think about how long they would stay and trade in Besh ba Gowah before leaving for Long River, and how many days it would take to get there. It would definitely be a long trip, but he could hardly wait to get started.

Brown Fox arrived back at the hut just after Gray Fawn had arrived with a small squirrel-skin bag clutched in her hand. She had just brushed the door hanging requesting entry, and Little Star pulled the door hanging aside asking Gray Fawn to enter. Understanding that the two sisters had many things to talk about, Brown Fox took a detour toward the center of the village, approaching the group of men discussing the situations at the village of Large House. He had seen Brave Beaver and Long Knife speaking with six other men, and Pretty Sky was hidden in the middle because of her shorter height. They were questioning her about the members of their families still living in the village of Large House, and she was doing her best to answer them as the questions were asked.

Gray Fawn handed the small squirrel-skin bag to Little Star and said, "Your brother, Red Wolf, left this with me and asked that I give it to you when you return to Besh ba Gowah. He knew that you would return someday, and wanted you to have the contents of this bag. He never told me what the bag contained, but I am sure that it was meaningful to him, and hopefully to you, too."

Little Star opened the bag and withdrew its contents: a white eagle feather, a bear claw, and a quartz stone that was formed in the form of a full white moon. These were items that reminded Red Wolf of his earlier life, from the seed of his birth father, chief Bear Claw, the moon stone representing White Moon, the woman who had helped raise him and who was Little Star's birth mother, and an eagle feather that helped him perform the duties of a shaman. These were the things that represented Red Wolf to Little Star, and she was thrilled to have these items to remember him by. Her next thoughts were to return them to Red Wolf when they next met, hopefully at the village of Long River in the not too distant future.

Then, it was time for conversation between the two sisters, Little Star and Gray Fawn. Little Star asked about Red Bird, Gray Fawn's mother, and was told that she had walked the path shortly after her sister Falling Star, chief Koko-Who-Travels' mother, had walked the path. She asked the questions so that she would not have to tell her story about Gray Eagle and Flying Eagle. She felt sure that she would not be able to tell her sister about the tragedies without breaking down in tears. But, after hearing of the passing of Falling Star and Red Bird, she relented and began to tell Gray Fawn what had happened.

She began, "It was one spring ago that Gray Eagle left Besh ba Lakado in a quest to visit a ledge that overlooks the huge valley and the lake that provides the water for our village. While he was on the quest, a cougar attacked from above and he was killed by the cougar. Gray Eagle's father, Straight Arrow, leader of the hunters of Besh ba Lakado, found his remains, and killed the cougar responsible for Gray Eagle's death. Gray Eagle's body was taken to the faraway ledge and placed there to watch over the lake, valley and village for all time. As for Flying Eagle, our second born son, he was picked up from the ground at a meadow and taken away from me by a huge eagle, and has never been returned. I had been told by my mother, White Moon, that Flying Eagle would be seen by many of our people flying above the earth, but I never could understand how that could be possible. Since Flying Eagle was taken away from me, I have heard stories from people who have seen the eagle-boy flying above them. I have not seen him, but people whom I have known and trust have told me they have seen him."

She could not go on and began to sob. Gray Fawn put her arm around Little Star and said, "I understand your grief. It is more than a mate and mother can bear. To lose two of your most loved people within such a short period of time is hard to understand, but the "Great One" has a plan for all of us. You must be aware of the stories that are being told around many campfires that the eagle-boy is the one who takes our praise and prayers to the "Great One" above. It is also said that the eagle-boy escorts the spirits of those who have walked the path to the "Great One's" happy hunting grounds. He has been seen by many people in villages that surround us, and they say his face shines as in brilliant sunlight, and his wings reach out as if to lift the spirits of those who have seen him." Knowing she had done what she could to lift the spirits of Little Star, Gray Fawn left the hut and walked to her own.

A short time later, Brown Fox returned to the hut and helped Little Star unpack some of the items that had been stacked inside the hut, and laid the sleeping mats down with the two larger mats on the ends with White Bear's in the middle. The two bird cages had already been set over in the corner of the hut, and the birds had begun "cooing" prior to eating their evening meal of berries and a few seeds found and picked up by Little Star beside the path under a prickly pear cactus. As they were working together, Brown Fox said to Little Star, "Pretty Sky was speaking with her mate, Brave Beaver, and her brother, Long Knife, about trying to rescue the women and children who still live in the village of Large House. She had said that their families were safe at the time she had fled, but she could not be sure they would remain that way. She told them that one of the five armed guards had been commanded to follow her and bring her back to Large House to be punished. After telling them of the attack by the wolves and the death of the man who had been following her, the men began talking about attacking their old home village and bringing the women and children to live with them at Besh ba Gowah. They had mentioned it may require men from this village to help in the rescue. It may be discussed tonight at the evening meal."

Little Star replied, "It would be difficult to rescue the women and children with the four remaining armed guards protecting the head man, Black Coyote. Perhaps they could be drawn away while the escape takes place. Black Coyote would never leave the protection of his big house and the walls surrounding him." Brown Fox agreed that it would be pretty hard to overpower the guards and lead the women and children to safety through the gates of the village of Large House without adding men from this village to help.

Just at that moment, a commotion arose outside the door of the hut, and a wild turkey darted into the hut through the open curtain, with many shouts of men and children who had chased the bird through the village. It had wandered in from the side opposite the brook, back where the trees opened up to the waterfall. The children were the first to spot the bird and began chasing it toward the center of the village. The men had heard the shouts and quickly began chasing the bird too. It had taken the first dark opening it had come to, coming to a halt in front of Brown Fox's left foot. It had nowhere to go, and Brown Fox bent over to grasp the turkey by the neck, giving it a quick twist, killing the bird. It was an old, big turkey hen with plenty of meat on its wide body. As the men and children stood outside of the hut honoring the privacy of Brown Fox and Little Star, Brown Fox walked to the doorway, clutching the dead turkey in his right hand. Seeing one of the hunters of the village standing to the side of the doorway, he handed the turkey to the man, and said, "This crazy old bird didn't see the hut into which it ran was already taken. I trust the meat will be good eating, and the feathers can become part of someone's garment or stuffing for a blanket or pillow."

The hunter replied, "This is an old turkey that will grace the pot of our cook for the evening meal tomorrow. You, Brown Fox, will have the first bite and your fill from this meal you have furnished to a good number of people in our village. We thank you for your gift of food, and all of us are looking forward to the trading in the village square tomorrow. Would you like to have the feathers of this turkey for trading? I would be happy to pluck the bird clean and return the feathers to you."

Brown Fox told the hunter, "No, I have given the turkey to you and you should have the opportunity to do with the feathers as you please. Perhaps your mate could find a use for the large ones as part of a warming blanket, while the small ones could be used as packing for a pillow. There are other uses we have seen in various villages we have passed through, but those are the most popular uses. If they were eagle feathers they would be most valued by your shaman, Gray Fawn, but the feathers of a turkey are valued only by those seeking warmth during a cold night or a soft pillow to lay their head upon."

One of the young girls of the village came over to the hut telling the men, children, and Brown Fox that the evening meal was ready to be eaten, and that all should go to the ceremonial pit for the special feast honoring the traveling traders. Brown Fox stepped back into the hut, asked Little Star whether she was ready to go to the feast, and they left the hut after letting the covering close behind them.

As they were passing one of the huts on the way to the ceremonial pit, White Bear came running toward them with a young boy about the same age chasing after him. It appeared they had been playing together and White Bear had the boy's wooden toy bear in his hands as he ran. Little Star gathered him up in her arms and looked White Bear straight in his eyes, saying, "White Bear, you must give your friend his toy bear back. You and he have been playing together and he let you play with his toy, but it is his toy. Give it back to him now, please."

White Bear looked at his mother, and knew from the look in her eyes the time for playing was over, and he handed the toy bear back down to his young friend. The boy took it from his hands, turned and ran back toward the hut in which he lived. As he reached the doorway, he turned and waved toward White Bear, as if to say without speaking, "Thank you for returning my bear and I hope to play with you again tomorrow."

Approaching the ceremonial pit, Little Star and Brown Fox noticed that little had changed except for the people who made up the circle in the middle. Chief Koko-Who-Travels and Gray Fawn had their son Eagle Wing propped up in a cradleboard between them with a handsome young man and apparently his mate sitting on the left side of the chief. To the right of Gray Fawn, a slightly older woman sat with a young boy next to her. The open spots opposite the chief and Gray Fawn were left for Little Star, Brown Fox and White Bear to sit. After they sat down, Gray Fawn rose and began a prayer of thanksgiving. "Oh "Great One," we thank You for bringing our good friends and family, Little Star, her son White Bear, and her partner Brown Fox, safely back to our village. We miss those who were with us the last time we gathered here, but we know they are safe within Your care at the village of Long River or with You in the happy hunting grounds. We also thank You for allowing us to use the foods that You and Mother Earth furnish us for our health and welfare. May we always remember that it is through Your help we are kept alive, and it is Your wish that we live in peace and harmony with other people You have placed around us."

There were a few glances around the outer circles of people as they heard the last part of Gray Fawn's prayer. Brave Beaver, Pretty Sky and Long Knife exchanged glances, and several of the men who had escaped from the village of Large House had also caught the words "we live in peace and harmony with other people you have placed around us." It was evident to them the meaning was a warning that it was not the time for them to bring up a war party to storm the walls of their former village of Large House in order to rescue the women and children remaining there as prisoners. It would be best to allow Little Star and Brown Fox to tell their stories this evening, and wait for another time to bring their own stories to this village gathering.

Chief Koko-Who-Travels began introducing the people around the inner circle and began with Little Star, explaining, "She is the sister of my mate, Gray Fawn, both fathered by the seed of the great traveling trader, Kokopelli. Little Star had twin sons birthed here in Besh ba Gowah just two fall seasons ago, and her son, White Bear, is sitting between her and her traveling trader-partner, Brown Fox. Her home village is Besh ba Lakado, many days journey toward the sundown direction. She is also the sister of our former shaman Red Wolf, who left the village one summer past to go to the village of Long River, the former home of his mate, Yellow Moon. Little Star will be telling the story of how her mate, Gray Eagle was killed, and her second son was taken from her."

He continued on, "Brown Fox is from a home village called Long River, the same village that Yellow Moon came from, and where she, Red Wolf and their daughter, Full Moon, began walking toward when they left our village of Besh ba Gowah. Brown Fox, Little Star, and White Bear are accompanied by the trained birds that fly between them and the wolves which pull their travois. They are very brave to face so many unknown dangers, but they have been very successful during their journeys."

He also introduced the remaining members of the inner circle, "Our leader of the hunters is Brave Hawk, and his mate, Green Stalk, is the leader of our gatherers. They both know the trails around our village for more than two days travel. The woman who sits next to my mate, Gray Fawn, is the teacher of this special young man who will one day become our shaman. The woman's name is Blue Stone, and the boy is Bright Sun. In a dream catcher that was shared by Gray Fawn, my mother, Falling

Star, and me, on three consecutive nights, we saw Bright Sun standing with his hands upraised in front of a huge animal with sharp horns lowered to the ground, its sides heaving from the exertion of running a great distance to arrive in front of Bright Sun. Bright Sun was talking to the animal and it was offering itself completely to Bright Sun. He laid hands on the head of the animal which fell over dead at his touch. The animal was so large that it fed the entire village for an entire ten days. The hide of the animal was so huge that it covered an entire hut. Soon, he will have learned all that Blue Stone can teach him, and it will be Gray Fawn who will begin teaching the functions of the shaman to Bright Sun. Depending on his learning, he should be our shaman in five summers, at his age of fourteen summers."

With the introductions having been made, the food was brought to the inner circle by four young girls. There were two pieces of venison, half of a squash, two small cobs of corn, and a sweet-tasting drink that had a blueberry flavor for each of the adults and Bright Sun in the circle, and a smaller portion for the young children.

After the food was eaten, the wooden plates were taken away by the serving girls. The chief rose, requesting quiet, then turning to Little Star asked, "Little Star, are you ready to tell us about what happened to your mate, Gray Eagle and your second son, Flying Eagle?" She agreed that it was time to let the members of the village know what happened.

Little Star began, "After leaving Besh ba Gowah just two winters past, Gray Eagle, Brown Fox, White Bear, Flying Eagle and I walked our way back to my home village of Besh ba Lakado, many days to the sundown direction. We arrived there and decided to stay the winter. We were offered the lookout's home above the lake and village, up in the cave where the hunters and gatherers live. It was a huge home compared to the huts below in the village, and had a beautiful view of the lake, village, the growing fields, and the mountains surrounding the valley. We lived in the lookout's home with Gray Eagle and Brown Fox taking turns watching over the entire valley. While watching from the beautiful spirit window, Gray Eagle spotted a ledge far above in the mountains in the sun-up direction that he wanted to visit in order to see the entire area from that ledge. After the snow melted enough for him to hike the trail safely, he left to visit that longed-for ledge. On the way there, he was attacked by a cougar and killed. Gray Eagle's father, Straight Arrow, head of the hunters of that village, led a group to find Gray Eagle, and they killed the cougar that had killed my mate, his son. They carried Gray Eagle's body to the ledge, placing it there to watch over the lake, mountains, valley and village for all time. The following summer, I took White Bear and Flying Eagle, my twin sons, out to a small meadow above the lake but down from the lookout's home. I had laid them on their tummies, and the largest eagle I have ever seen swooped down and picked up Flying Eagle in its talons and flew off and disappeared over the mountains across the lake and valley. People have claimed to have seen the eagle-boy, Flying Eagle, flying high above them, and I have seen him in my dream catchers, too. But, I have been told that I would never hold my son in my arms again. He has been taken by the "Great One" and has been given a special mission which will continue on for all time." While telling the story, she broke down in sobs a number of times, and at the end, she fell to her knees on the ground and cried out her grief.

The members of the village had listened to Little Star's story, and it was evident from the looks on their faces, they felt sorry for her. It was terrible to lose a mate while being so young, but to lose a son, especially a twin son who had lived for just under a full year, was tragic. To have lost both of them in such a short period of time was unimaginable. Many of the villagers had known and respected Gray Eagle, and had been living there when the twin sons, White Bear and Flying Eagle, were born. The crowd was stunned to silence, and it took Brown Fox to break the mood by getting up and helping Little Star to her feet, accompanying her to their hut, with White Bear following behind.

As they were leaving, chief Koko-Who-Travels cleared his throat, and his mate, Gray Fawn, said, "May the "Great One" ease your pain, and lighten your grief. Our village of Besh ba Gowah recognizes the great distress you carry with you, and will try to make your stay here as peaceful and pleasant as possible. We will prepare the trading place for your use at sun-up, but take your time in preparing yourselves and your products for the time you will want to begin trading."

Little Star turned and acknowledged Gray Fawn's words by saying, "Thank you Gray Fawn, and all of you, for your understanding of my despair and sorrow in telling the story." With that, she, Brown Fox and White Bear resumed their walk toward the safety of the hut.

Upon entering the hut, Brown Fox assisted Little Star by holding her arm as she sank down onto her sleeping mat, curling up in a fetal position and continuing to sob.

CHAPTER 3

After Little Star, Brown Fox and White Bear had left the ceremonial pit, and a short silence for meditation was observed, chief Koko-Who-Travels told the villagers that the trading area would be set-up the following morning just after sunrise, and trading would begin when Little Star and Brown Fox readied their products for display. He then asked if there was any other business to be discussed before leaving for their huts for the night.

Brave Beaver rose from his cross-legged seated position and said, "Chief Koko-Who-Travels, men and women of Besh ba Gowah, I ask that you hear what my mate, Pretty Sky, from the village of Large House, has to say about the plight of the women and children who still live there. As you know, I, my brother Long Knife, and six other men escaped from that village three summers past and arrived here two summers past, becoming members of this village."

Chief Koko-Who-Travels spoke saying, "You are invited to speak, Pretty Sky."

Pretty Sky stood and began to tell her story, "The village of Large House is ruled by chief Black Coyote, who arrived at our village seven summers past with five huge armed men to do his bidding. He killed the chief we had at that time, took over the big house, demanding the men of the village go out and bring back large branches from trees that would become horizontal braces for enlarging the height of his house. He held the women and children captive inside the walls of the village while the men went out to find, cut, and carry the large limbs back to the village where the straight limbs were set into the walls. Caliche mud taken from the clay beneath the soil was mixed with water, then formed and hardened as it dried into higher walls. The women were told when to plant, weed, and harvest the crops, and were punished by the five armed men if we did not do as we were told. When our men escaped, the work and punishments were more severe. Little Star and Brown Fox can verify that what I say is true. Chief Black Coyote is not a good chief, taking the food we planted and harvested for himself and his five guards. When I escaped, he sent one of the guards to try to catch me and bring me back for punishment. Instead I was saved; the wolves of Little Star and Brown Fox found the guard in a wash outside of their camp. I had collapsed near a large cropping of rocks not far from the wash, and was awakened when the wolves attacked and killed the guard. It would be my hope that my mate, Brave Beaver, my brother, Long Knife, the six other men who escaped with them, and perhaps a few of the men of Besh ba Gowah, could go and help the women and children who remain in the village of Large House to escape. The lives we led while working and starving at the will of chief Black Coyote and his guards were not lives of peace and harmony, but of toil, strife and eventual starvation. I am asking the villagers of Besh ba Gowah to aid in rescuing the families who still live in the village of Large House."

Sitting down next to Brave Beaver after finishing speaking, Pretty Sky looked around at the circle of stunned faces. The residents of Besh ba Gowah had heard of the village of Large House, and the leader was said to be the most clever man in the world. How could it be that he was such a despot? How could he have brought five armed men into a village, killed the chief, and taken over the village without being challenged? Was it their place to interfere with a village so far away? However, Brave Beaver, Long Knife and the six other men who had fled the village of Large House and become residents of Besh ba Gowah, were strong, responsible residents of their village now, and greatly missed their families they had abandoned. None had ever mated in this village, although there were several opportunities for them to have done so in the past.

Chief Koko-Who-Travels stood up and began speaking. "Residents of Besh ba Gowah, this is a situation that demands our combined thoughts and comments, not one that can be quickly resolved. Peace and harmony is what we have lived by, and conflict has not been a part of our lives. I believe that we should think this situation over, discuss it among ourselves, and meet again tomorrow evening when we can decide on a wise course of action. As for now, please allow my mate, Gray Fawn, our village shaman, to offer a prayer to the "Great One" asking for wisdom and courage to arrive at the correct decision."

Shaman Gray Fawn stood after chief Koko-Who-Travels sat down. She raised her hands in front of her, beseeching the people of the village to follow her lead, and praying aloud, "Oh "Great One," please listen to our hearts and minds while we consider the situation of which we have just become aware. The families of the men who have been a part of our Besh ba Gowah village for almost a full year are threatened by a man and his armed guards who prey on the weakness of the women and children still living in the village of Large House. Please give us an indication of what we must do to make things right in Your eyes. Conflict is not a part of our lives, so please lead us to a solution where we can remain true to peace and harmony in our lives, and direct us to find a way to help those who need our help."

With that prayer being offered to the "Great One," the people of the inner circle rose and began to walk toward their huts. The people of the outer circle stood as chief Koko-Who-Travels and shaman Gray Fawn, who was carrying their son Eagle Wing, passed through the opening leading to their hut. Brave Hawk and Green Stalk left next, followed by Blue Stone and Bright

Sun. There had been silence until Blue Stone and Bright Sun had left the outer circle and begun their longer walk toward the downside of the brook, where they would observe the skies before going to the hut in which the two lived.

The silence turned to many questions asked of the eight men and Pretty Sky, all of them concerning their families and their escapes from the village of Large House. "How far is Large House from here?" "How long did it take you to find our village after you escaped?" "How many women and children were living there when you left?" Each question was answered by the men as best they could, but Pretty Sky was the person with the most recent and reliable information. She had told them, "There have been some residents who walked the path since the men left, but there were two births and one escape that took place since then. In fact, the mate of Long Knife gave birth to a son after his escape, and his name is Gray Squirrel. He is the same age as White Bear, the trader Little Star's son."

Other questions were what Brave Beaver, Long Knife, Pretty Sky and the other men expected of the members of Besh ba Gowah, and how the women and children could be rescued without violence. Could trades be made with the chief of Large House that would release the people from the slavery they were living under? Knowing that there were no firm answers that could be determined at this time, one by one the group broke up and walked back to their huts for the evening. Brave Beaver and Pretty Sky stayed together for a longer time, catching up on the personal things that they had been keeping in their hearts and minds during their absence from each other. The two of them walked over to the brook hand-in-hand, whispering their longing for each other, and finally searching out a grassy spot on which to lie down and visit the moon and stars together. The moon seemed to smile down at them, and the stars surrounded and held them close as they neared the release they had both dreamed of for such a long time. Lying there in each others arms, they renewed their love and needs in whispers that remained in that small space of grass next to the brook and in their memories for all time.

The following morning, just before sun-up, Brave Hawk and some of his hunters set-up the stumps and woven branch covers in the area that was used for trading. The trading area had been expanded since Gray Eagle and Brown Fox had traded there while Little Star had delivered the twin boys two late-summers ago. There were now four stumps with three covers where the trade goods would be displayed, and a small area near the center in which the goods to be traded by the residents of Besh ba Gowah would be accepted or rejected by Brown Fox or Little Star. Any questioned trades would be judged by chief Koko-Who-Travels. All was ready for the arrival and set-up of trade goods by the two traveling traders.

Brown Fox woke up first, and gently woke White Bear. It would be a perfect time to take him out to the brook for taking a quick cool bath before waking Little Star. He also released the three wolves from the tether to which they had been fastened, and they all went toward the brook together. Little Star had wakened when the door covering was drawn aside, but had not shown any sign of being awake as the young man and her son left the hut. She thought to herself, 'Brown Fox is learning the ways of being a father even though he is not the father of White Bear. He will be a great father when his time comes. I must let him be of service to the women of the villages we enter to trade with. He is of the age that his seed can become a son or daughter to some of the women who need to help increase the number of residents in the villages in which they live. I will speak with Gray Fawn about this if we can have a few moments alone today. I am certain that he is ready to enjoy the company of a nice young woman who can teach him the path to the moon and stars.'

It was time for Little Star to get up and ready herself for a quick morning bath and prepare the trading goods to be taken to the area that had already been set up. The travois poles were standing against the back of the hut, so she went back to bring them to the front and positioned them for loading.

Brown Fox, White Bear, and the three wolves returned to the hut just as the loading had been started, so Little Star went down to the brook for her bath and Brown Fox took over the loading of the travois while White Bear played with the wolves. As the last of the trading goods were loaded onto the travois, Little Star returned from the brook looking as if the issues of the night before were all washed away during her bath, and she was looking forward to the challenges of becoming a shrewd but fair trader again.

The pulling harness was placed over the young female wolf's shoulders, through its front legs, around to the back and tied securely. Then, Little Star and Brown Fox each lifted one of the long ends of the travois poles, inserted them into the loops that were then tightened, and everything was in readiness to be dragged into the trading area. As they passed by some of the huts along the way, people began coming out of their huts to see what items they might need to trade for, and think about the items they may offer in trade for those items. By the time they reached the trading area, there were five women who were following the travois, just waiting to be the first traders for the day. Clothing including breechcloths, footwear, and headbands were laid out first, with woven baskets, jewelry, flints, pottery, shells, carved dolls and seashells being the other items offered on the woven blankets spread over the leafy branches. Carved wooden bowls, cups, and scoops would be other items this village would be happy to trade for as well.

The trading began when one of the first five women who had been following Little Star and Brown Fox's party, grabbed a nicely softened and sewn pair of rabbit-fur moccasins, offering an elaborately-carved squirrel standing on its back legs with an acorn held up to its mouth in its front paws. It had been highly polished with animal fats and shone in the sunlight to a beautiful deep brown color. This was a very good trade for both traders, filling a need for one and offering a beautiful piece of art for a future trade to the other. From that time on through most of the day trading was brisk and profitable. Chief Koko-Who-Travels, Gray Fawn, Brave Beaver, Pretty Sky, and many others passed before the offerings, with Brave Beaver trading some beaver pelts to Little Star for a stone bracelet with a turquoise stone imbedded in the middle top. This was given immediately to Pretty Sky, who smiled widely as she put it on her left wrist. Other significant trades were made, but Little Star took great satisfaction with Brave Beaver's trade as being the best of the day. As the trading day came to an end, the trading goods were loaded onto the travois and taken back to the hut where Brown Fox and Little Star were staying. While Brown Fox unloaded the travois and put things into the hut, Little Star went to seek out Gray Fawn for the talk she had prepared concerning Brown Fox and a woman to show him the way to the moon and stars. It certainly could not be Little Star, although she had a deep affection for him. He was several years younger than her, she did not have a mate, but her heart and mind still clung to the memories of Gray Eagle. No, she just could not be the person to show him the way!

Little Star found Gray Fawn outside the hut in which she and her mate, chief Koko-Who-Travels, lived. Gray Fawn was tying up some watercress leaves she had found after following the brook upstream for half a day. Seeing Little Star approach, she said, "Hello sister Little Star! I am hopeful that your trading went well today, and helped take away some of the pain and suffering you endured last evening. Is there anything I can help you with, or did you come over to talk? Let's sit down for awhile out here in the sunshine and just relax and talk."

After sitting down together, Little Star began to tell Gray Fawn her thoughts of having Brown Fox introduced to the wondrous flight to the moon and stars. She began by saying, "Gray Fawn, I believe it is time to introduce Brown Fox to a woman who may take him on his first flight to the moon and stars. He is a very young man who can produce many seeds and help increase the number of new members to each village we travel. As a traveling trader, it has been customary that we leave behind more than traded goods, and it encourages traders to return to villages in which they have offered growth. Is there a young woman within Besh ba Gowah who would be helpful in such a task?"

Gray Fawn had listened to Little Star's request, but said nothing at first. Her mind was going over the words that had been said, and she didn't know how or what to answer. She, herself, had never been asked, nor had she considered, visiting the moon and stars until chief Koko-Who-Travels asked her to become his mate. After assisting her mother Red Bird in delivering the babies of the women of the village, she had not wanted the pain associated with the delivery of a child, until she was mated to her childhood friend. To bring forth another life, one whose seed was from the man whom she loved deeply, changed her mind. She was now the mother of Eagle Wing, a child who was a combination of Koko-Who-Travels and her, by the grace of the "Great One." The pain was great, but the blessings were greater. How should she answer the request? Was there something that she could say that might help piece together the life of her sister, Little Star, and suggest that she, rather than another woman, be the one to introduce Brown Fox to the moon and stars, and bring those fantastic feelings of love and belonging back to her own life? Would Brown Fox accept such a wonderful gift? Would it be a need or a want for him? And, would it soothe the heart and mind of Little Star as they traveled together over the many expected summers ahead? No answers came without questions that raced through Gray Fawn's mind, but she replied, "It is such an important journey, that first one. Are you sure that it should be a stranger who travels with Brown Fox? He is such a caring and capable father-figure to White Bear, and he takes good care of you and the wolves. He must have feelings for you, more than just as a partner who will eventually lead him back to his home village of Long River, and to see his first love, Yellow Moon, your brother Red Wolf's mate. He learned much from you and Gray Eagle during your times together, and I know that he mourns the loss of Gray Eagle deeply. Before possibly losing a valuable friend and partner to another, you might ask him to become your mate, if not by the mating ceremony, at least by introducing the flight between the both of you. You may never recapture the love and feelings you had for Gray Eagle, but give yourself and Brown Fox the opportunity to teach each other the places and things that make you happy, and maybe they will be all that you both would seek."

This was not what Little Star expected to hear when she sought out the thoughts and wisdom of her sister, Gray Fawn. What was Gray Fawn thinking? How could she ever think that Brown Fox could compare to the love and contentment Little Star had known while mated to Gray Eagle? This was not possible, or was it? Did she dare to suggest such a thing to Brown Fox? How would she arrange it? It would be exciting to once more feel arms around her, holding her close, feeling another heart beat against her own breasts. She flushed for a moment thinking how much she missed the touch of another person. It was wonderful to feel White Bear in her arms, or having his arms wrapped around her neck, but it was not the same as when Gray Eagle touched her, anywhere on her body. That was what she missed, and there was no doubt about it. She hadn't given that special feeling a thought for so long, and now it came flooding back to her. But, it would not be the same, or would it? Hurriedly, she rose from her sitting position and said her thank you and good-bye to Gray Fawn, striding quickly back to the hut in which Brown Fox and she would share, along with White Bear. Yes, she thought, White Bear would witness the flight, but would he realize what was happening?

Pushing the flap to the side, she entered the hut and saw that the sleeping mats had been rolled up and were now standing in the corner next to the empty bird cages. There were the two large mats, and the smaller one. Apparently, Brown Fox had done the cleaning, and had taken the birds out for flying, and gone to talk with other young men in the village square. He certainly did take care of the things they both had to do, and offered a lot of help in their everyday living. And, he was very good with White Bear taking him with him when he had to do things like gather wood for fires, get the water bags filled, or even taking him for baths and relieving themselves. He was young, but very aware of what had to be done, and willing to do more than his share. Yes, he had earned the right to be a man, and it was only right that she show him she appreciated and cared for the attention he had shown her, White Bear, and Gray Eagle. She felt strange as she picked up the larger of the two sleeping mats, placing it on the left side of the hut. She placed the second in the middle, with the small mat for White Bear on the end. It was then she realized that Brown Fox had grown quite a lot since he joined Gray Eagle and her after they left Long River. He was actually taller than her now, and his back and arms had filled out and become strong. He had become a man, a good man, and she was beginning to realize that he was more than a partner in the trading business.

Just then, the flap opened and Brown Fox walked in with a bird on each of his arms, followed by White Bear. He looked down at the sleeping mats as he walked around them to the cages, not saying a word. He was not aware of the conversation held between Gray Fawn and Little Star, but was puzzled as to why Little Star's sleeping pad was next to his rather than on the other side of White Bear's. He looked at Little Star quizzically, but again remained silent. She was momentarily embarrassed, turning her eyes away briefly, as she said, "I thought tonight we might have White Bear sleep on the other side of me if that is acceptable to you." Brown Fox agreed, but said no more. It was time to go to the ceremonial pit for evening meal, and the three left the hut together. They watched as the children of the village were playing with the wolves, grabbing their tails, wagging them, and then running while the wolves chased them. It looked like great fun, and White Bear wanted to join in the fun, but it was time to eat.

The seating for the meal was the same as the night before, with chief Koko-Who-Travels, Gray Fawn, Eagle Wing, Brave Hawk, Green Stalk, Blue Stone, Bright Sun, Little Star, Brown Fox and White Bear making up the inner circle with the much larger circle being the rest of the villagers. After the meal was finished, chief Koko-Who-Travels stood up and addressed the village saying, "We have had time to think about the words of Pretty Sky, and consider the people remaining in the village of Large House. We should have come up with some ideas as to what our position should be in this matter. Do any of you have ideas that you want to express?"

Brave Hawk, head of the hunters for the village of Besh ba Gowah stood and was recognized by the chief. Brave Hawk said, "It is my thought that we could drive a few deer toward the village of Large House and let the lookout see the availability of venison, something they do not eat regularly. This might bring the armed guards out of the village long enough to allow the women and children time to escape while the guards try to catch the deer. In this way, we could help without disturbing our peaceful and harmonious way of life." He then sat down.

Many of the villagers nodded their agreement of the plan, but just then Bright Sun stood up and seemed to be in a trance. He began speaking, "I see a great dust storm rising in the direction of the hot winds. The storm is so intense no one can see through the clouds of dust. The winds blow so hard that whirling winds pick up the guards who stand at the gate to the village of Large House. The storm will arrive there in eleven days. There is time for the men who came from that village to go back and bring their families to us if they leave at sun-up tomorrow. The way there will be in a direct line over the mountains with the dripping springs. Lie in wait until you hear the screech of the eagle boy who will lead the storm to the gates of the village of Large House. The chief of the village will be hiding inside the walls of his big house, and will not hear the sound of you leading the women and children to safety. Long Knife, please come before me so that I can lay my hands of protection on your shoulders. You will lead the men back to the village of Large House and escort your families to the safety of your new homes here."

Long Knife approached the inner circle and stooped over before Bright Sun, who placed his hands upon the shoulders of Long Knife. Bright Sun said, "Long Knife, be brave and escort your mate, Star Watcher and your son, Gray Squirrel, and all of the other members of the people enslaved by Black Coyote, to the safety of our village."

With that, Bright Sun slumped to the ground. Blue Stone, his teacher and protector knelt beside him, and poured some water over his fevered brow. He woke as though nothing had happened, but it was a short period of time nobody that was there that evening ever forgot. He was the appointed one, the new shaman of Besh ba Gowah.

The entire village was amazed at the outcome of the meeting about the village of Large House. The outcome had been decided by one of the youngest of the village, and the finality of the decision was immediate. With the decision having been made, the people rose and returned to their huts. The men who were to leave the next sun-up had things to pack: food, clothing and sleeping mats. Some were hunters and packed their bows, arrows, knives and spears to take with them. This was not thought to be a hike, but a long walk of nine days in the hot sun, at least. This was to be a quest to become whole with their families again.

As for the rest of the villagers, it would be a night of prayers to the "Great One" for their friends who were going on a mission to bring their families to a new home in Besh ba Gowah. New homes would have to be built so that all of the families would have places to live. Additional food sources would have to be found and collected. New faces, families, friends would arrive and bloodlines would expand.

Brown Fox, Little Star and White Bear walked to the brook to get a clearer view of the sunset before heading back to the hut. Little Star was thinking of how she would approach the delicate issue of inviting Brown Fox into the quest for the moon and stars. What would she do? How should she start? What if he would not want the affection she planned to bestow upon him? The thoughts raced through her mind, but there was no clear plan that emerged. She knew that he knew the sleeping mats were arranged differently, but did he know why? Would he make a move, or was it her that would have to begin the traveling? At last, a plan formed in her mind and she asked, "Brown Fox, would you like to swim with White Bear and me? It would be exciting to take a swim in the evening under the moon and stars. The water is not too cool and the air is warm. I am sure that it would do wonders for us before we go to seek our dream catchers. Will you walk upstream a little way so that we can swim in privacy?"

He answered, "If that is what you would like to do, then I am pleased to go with you. It will be a perfect night to see the moon and many stars." As they arrived at the side of the brook, Little Star stripped off the breechcloth from White Bear's torso, and began undressing herself. It was not unusual for Brown Fox to see Little Star naked in the lookout's post at Besh ba Lakado while Gray Eagle, Little Star and he had lived together there. But after Gray Eagle had walked the path, Little Star and the twin boys moved to his father and mother, Straight Arrow and Yellow Bird's, cave dwelling. He had not seen her without clothes since then.

Brown Fox stripped off his breechcloth and waded into the water up to his knees, then waited for Little Star and White

Bear to enter. White Bear squealed as the cool water tickled his feet when Little Star carried him in until she too was knee deep. The sun was setting beyond the tree line with the shadows just touching the top leaves of the trees to the right of where they had entered the water. The darkness would soon reveal the many stars, and the moon had already made its entry into the sky just behind those tree tops. Little Star turned toward Brown Fox, lowering White Bear from where she had held him against her breasts, and she began to bend over to swing him between her legs. White Bear seemed to enjoy the dipping and Little Star was happy to show her breasts to an increasingly curious young Brown Fox. Brown Fox had never seen anything like this before, and he began to crouch down in the water to hide an evident result of the show he was watching. Brown Fox was unsure to what extent his duties and commitment were to Little Star. He did know that she was a desirable young woman, older than him, but still a young woman. He had been with Gray Eagle and Little Star when they had traveled to the moon and stars together, but he had never asked, nor been asked by anyone to make the trip before. It was all he could do to keep from staring at Little Star, treasuring the view, as he had never taken the time, nor had the interest, to watch the young girls he had seen in the water at the villages they had visited since he joined Gray Eagle and Little Star.

Slowly she moved over closer to where Brown Fox was crouched in the water, and indicated by actions that she wanted him to stand and take White Bear, swinging him as she was doing. He rose from the crouch and took White Bear, swinging him just as Little Star had been doing. Watching the two of them enjoying the dipping and swinging, Little Star saw that the effect she had hoped for had occurred and Brown Fox had become aroused. In a few moments they were sitting next to each other in the water next to the bank with Little Star between Brown Fox and White Bear. She put her arms tenderly around each of them, and began rubbing Brown Fox's back. He had never felt the touch of a woman as soft and as lovingly as Little Star's touch. It was all he needed to reach over and caress her left breast with the inside palm of his left hand. It was a hand that had known work, rough but careful not to scratch or hurt the delicate breast he was touching. He was fearful at first that she might pull away, but it seemed that she offered more of herself to him. White Bear tired of sitting in the water, and began to fuss so Brown Fox and Little Star decided it was time to take him back to the hut. They had spent very little time watching the moon and the twinkling stars during the time they were in the water, but they knew that there would be many more nights during which that could be done. After putting on their clothes, they walked back into the village.

Arriving at the hut, they found that someone had tethered the wolves to an exposed root next to the doorway, but out of the way if someone wanted entry. The wolves were resting comfortably, probably dreaming of all of the exercise they had gotten from playing with the children of the village.

Brown Fox pushed the curtain to the side allowing Little Star and White Bear to enter ahead of him. A small twig lit by two flints that Brown Fox carried, lit the interior of the hut long enough for all three of them to ready themselves for their sleeping mats. Carefully, Little Star bent over and gave White Bear a loving kiss on his cheek, then turned to give a startled Brown Fox a deep loving kiss on his lips. She turned and lay down on her sleeping mat, turning toward the sleeping mat of Brown Fox. The light was blown out, and Brown Fox lay down on his sleeping mat, turning toward Little Star. He was unsure of what to do next, so he asked, "Little Star, do I have your permission to become one with you this night, or have I misjudged your indications to me. I have never journeyed to the moon and stars with anyone, so please help me become a real man in your eyes and heart."

Little Star answered, "Through your caring, feelings and working with Gray Eagle, White Bear, and me, you have become a real man in my eyes and heart already. I have learned to respect and honor you, and will admit to loving you from afar. Now it is time to find our way together to the moon and stars. Please join with me." With that, the journey began.

CHAPTER 4

The following sun-up, the village was up and anxious to bid goodbyes and good luck wishes to the men who were going to the village of Large House in order to bring their families and friends to Besh ba Gowah. A friend of Brave Beaver and Long Knife, Blue Nose, decided to go along with the group and try to help carry items that might be too heavy for the others to carry alone. He was a tall, thin man, whose eyesight was the best of the entire village. It was he who could spot a chicken hawk diving from above toward a lonely rabbit as many as ten tree lengths away, and it was he who could spot the village of Large House before the lookout could spot their approach. Everybody agreed it was a good addition to the group. Food and water bags were sent with the men and shouts of encouragement and prayers were heard as they walked away toward the distant mountains.

Brown Fox and White Bear went down to the brook, followed by the wolves which had been loosened from their tether by Brown Fox. They were not the first to have gone down to the brook as they met Brave Hawk and Green Stalk returning from a quick dip in the refreshing water. As they met on the pathway, Brave Hawk said, "You Brown Fox are a lucky man to be able to travel from one end of the world to the other. We who live in a village never get to see what the great waters in the sundown direction look like, or the never-ending sands in the sun-up direction. What do you find as the most interesting part of the world you have seen?"

Brown Fox answered, "Brave Hawk, the love of a man and woman, the inside of a warm, comfortable hut, children who are growing into young people, and a meal of whatever food and water available in a village, is all a person needs to be happy."

Brave Hawk replied, "You speak with more experience than your years. It is good that you accompany Little Star, as she is our favorite traveling trader. She has brought more good happenings to this village than any other traveler. We respect you and her and hope that we will see you many more times in the future. Will you be leaving Besh ba Gowah later today or at sun-up tomorrow?"

Brown Fox said, "We will be leaving at sun-up tomorrow. We have decided to follow Little Star's brother, Red Wolf, and his mate, Yellow Moon, to her and my home village, Long River. It will be a long and hard walk of at least fifteen days, but we are hopeful of finding them, along with my mother and father, in good health."

With that, the friends parted. Brown Fox, White Bear and the wolves walked to the brook, while Brave Hawk and Green Stalk returned to the village. As they walked toward the water, Brown Fox was remembering the excitement he had felt when Little Star had bent over and begun swinging White Bear between her legs and dipping him in the water. He was reliving each movement that Little Star and he had made from that point to climbing each step toward the faraway moon and stars, and finally the point at which he had felt his seed leave his body and enter hers. He had been told that this was a great gift the "Great One" had given to both men and women, and he was sure that it had to be the greatest gift next to life itself.

There were a number of villagers who were gathering around the hut of the master builder for the village, and he was asking for help in building some new huts for the expected arrival of the families from the village of Large House. His plan was to build seven new huts which were to be built at the edge of the village nearest the path to the sun-up direction. Five men and four of the women volunteered to help. The men were asked to do the digging, carrying and mixing of the rock and sand with the water the women would bring from the brook. Brave Hawk had gathered three of his best hunters together to plan for a hunt that would take them to an area in which deer and mountain sheep were often found as they would need additional food when the new families arrived. Green Stalk was already talking with Gray Fawn and planning to go on a gathering trip for berries, herbs, mushrooms, nuts, tobacco leaves, and watercress. This was going to be a very busy and growing village for a long time. Today would be busy for Brown Fox and Little Star and would be spent packing up the travois, giving bulky items to members of the village who could use them, and saying the goodbyes to all of the villagers they met as everyone hurried to accomplish their day's work.

White Bear knew that they were leaving, and took the opportunity to take the wolves with him to play with the friends he had made. Little Star went over to chief Koko-Who-Travels and Gray Fawn's hut, enjoying the time she spent with her sister and Green Stalk. Chief Koko-Who-Travels had left to check on the plans being made by the master builder and the hunters to make sure he understood them. Eagle Wing was suckling his breakfast when Little Star first arrived, then was laid down for a nap after drinking his fill. The talk turned to the best wishes to be conveyed to Red Wolf, Yellow Moon and Full Moon at the village of Long River, and the hopes that the trip would be a safe and easy one for the travelers.

After Green Stalk left the hut, Little Star began telling Gray Fawn that she had been correct in encouraging her to resume her life. She told of the wonderful flight to the moon and stars with Brown Fox. She told her that later, during her dream catcher, Gray Eagle had come to her and told her that she should continue to live her life as a woman, not only as a traveling trader, but a complete woman with a man at her side, if she wanted or needed. He had said, "A woman is not to be alone, just as a man is not to be alone. That is why the "Great One" created both, giving them the great gift of the moon and stars. Children are not given to those who travel to the moon and stars alone. You have time to become a mother again." With that, he came close, kissed her, and was gone. Little Star asked Gray Fawn, "You are a shaman, a woman of the "Great One." What do you think Gray Eagle meant when he said I should be a complete woman, with a man by my side, if I want or need one? I had never traveled to the moon and stars with another man until last night with Brown Fox. Brown Fox has been a great friend and helper, enjoys being with White Bear, and is very kind and considerate of me. I do love him for those reasons, but is that enough? Or should I look for another? I am so unsure of what I want or need."

Gray Fawn had listened intently to the words of Little Star, but sought some of the feelings behind the words that Little Star had spoken. She felt that Little Star had a great appreciation for the things that Brown Fox could do and did for her, but was this the man for her? Just as importantly, was she the woman for him? This was something that could not be answered by Gray Fawn, and she was wise enough to know that any answer she might give at that moment may or may not stand the test of time. She said, "Little Star, there is nothing I can tell you that your heart does not know. Your heart and mind will tell you over time. Life is for the living, and the visit in your dream catcher by Gray Eagle releases you from the bond to him who is no longer of this world. Live your life as your heart directs. You are not evil if your heart directs you to another, but remember Brown Fox is a known person. You have seen him as a friend, a partner, and have shown him the way to the moon and stars for the very first time. Also remember, it is he that must return the love and caring that are behind that trip. To say that you accept him is not to say that he accepts you. This must be said and lived between two people, not just one. Go now, and think over what we have discussed. It is time to pray for guidance from the "Great One" and think about tomorrow as well as today."

After thanking Gray Fawn, Little Star gave her a hug, and turned to leave. Her heart was singing as she left the hut of chief Koko-Who-Travels and Gray Fawn, hurrying back to the hut that she, Brown Fox and White Bear had slept in, saying the goodbyes and wishing well to the passersby. Arriving at the hut, Little Star saw that the bird cages were empty and that most of the things they would be taking with them the following day were packed and ready to be strapped onto the travois. Brown Fox had been working at preparing for their departure, and had taken White Bear and the wolves with him to exercise the birds.

The midday meal was being served and Little Star joined a group of women, which included Pretty Sky, who had been a particularly active trader during the trading session the day before. Pretty Sky had had nothing of her own with which to trade. However, Brave Beaver and Long Knife, her mate and her brother, were hunters, and had been awarded pelts of animals they had brought into the village. The two men gave Pretty Sky some of the pelts which she traded for items that would help to equip their hut to her liking. She had been very active in trading for those types of items. The other women had kept Brown Fox and Little Star busy with their trades for clothing, footwear and jewelry.

Fry bread and small pieces of boiled quail meat were eaten, and the conversation quickly turned to the men who had left to bring back the families from the village of Large House. Everyone in the village of Besh ba Gowah was praying for and counting on the safe return of the men and the families they would bring with them. Following that, Little Star thanked the women for their great trades and hoped that all of them received what was needed in return. When Little Star stood up and readied herself to leave, the group all stood up as well and exchanged brief hugs with Little Star. The last, and most meaningful hug was from Pretty

Sky who thanked Little Star for saving her life, bringing her to this village and returning her to her mate. They all said, "Until we meet again, be well, and safe travels!"

There were whoops and hollers as Brown Fox, White Bear, the wolves and birds returned from their flying outing. The male wolf brought back a large rabbit in its mouth, dropping it in front of the hut that Brown Fox, Little Star and White Bear were using. The wolf turned aside as Brown Fox picked up the rabbit and carried it inside the hut. White Bear remained outside with the wolves, playfully rubbing the tops of their heads and their ears. Brown Fox returned outside with the rabbit in one hand and a knife to cut up the rabbit in the other. Sitting down just to the left of the doorway in the shade of a small spruce tree, he began to slice the underside of the rabbit from the throat to tail, then peeled back the brown-gray pelt from the meat underneath. A young boy about eight summers old came over to watch Brown Fox, and then two other younger boys joined the first. As he finished separating the pelt from the meaty part inside, Brown Fox laid the pelt over a small boulder. Next, he scraped the meat from the bones from the neck down toward the tail, leaving the legs attached to the carcass. The meat was laid on a piece of woven reed mat, after which Brown Fox gave the carcass, including some meat clinging to the bones, to the male wolf. Then, he took the meat to the brook to be washed before cutting it into small pieces to be fried and used as traveling food.

The evening meal was eaten quietly as there were many of the villagers that had gone with the hunters and gatherers as well as the men who had left for the village of Large House. Those who were still in the village waited quietly for the chief to rise and bid goodbye to the departing traveling traders with Gray Fawn saying a short prayer to the "Great One" on behalf of her sister, Little Star, Brown Fox, White Bear, the birds, and the wolves that helped carry their precious trading items. Little Star rose and thanked everyone for their good trades, their prayers, and well wishes. She promised to return to visit again in the future. With that being said, everyone made their way back to their huts, and prepared for their dream catchers.

Little Star was unsure of what would happen as she lay next to Brown Fox. Would he turn over toward her? Would he speak, inviting conversation? Would he reach out to touch her? Or, would he turn away from her, reject any conversation, or rebuff any advances she would make toward him if nothing else happened?

Brown Fox had questions in his mind too. Was it his duty, was he expected to say or do anything? He knew that he had a new respect for Little Star, and wanted to take another trip to the moon and stars with her. But, what if she did not appreciate the trip the night before? What if he had done something to offend her, or he had done something wrong? He took a chance and said, "Little Star, I want to thank you for last night. It honored me greatly that you and I visited the moon and stars together, and me for the first time. I ask you, did you appreciate the trip as much as I did? Did I do things that pleased you, as you did for me? I really want to know if there is something more I can do to fulfill your happiness as you did mine."

Little Star had her answers. He had been honored by her attentions. She had made him aware of her as more than a partner, and mother to White Bear. It was too early to tell if she should be committed entirely to him, or him to her, but it was a start. She reached over to him with her right hand and cupped the left side of his face, rubbing it gently and said, "Brown Fox, it was me that felt honored that you found me attractive enough to allow me to be the first to travel to the moon and stars with you. We will have many days and nights together while we travel to your home village, Long River. I can't expect that you will want me to remain with you beyond that time, but I will tell you this; you are a man now, and able to plant seed for children. You will meet many women over your lifetime, and none will honor you, rely and respect you, more than me. I thank you deeply for the love you have shown me and White Bear. I invite you to become a part of me as we travel, and time will tell if we are to be mated by the mating ceremony." With that, she withdrew her hand to see if he had ideas of his own. Yes, he did! Love filled her heart, body and mind again!

CHAPTER 5

Sun-up was a rosy red sky instead of the golden rays of sunshine, meaning that there could be a dust storm heading their way. Brown Fox and Little Star had prepared for three weather possibilities–hot sun, rain, or clouds. The dust storm possibility was something new for them as they needed clothing that would cover their faces, and the rest of their bodies, while still being cool. The blowing sand could sting the skin, blind the eyes and plug the nose, but they could wait until they met the storm, or maybe it wasn't out there at all. They decided to wear the clothes for the cloudy weather, and have the coverings for their bodies and faces strapped separately on the top of the travois.

As they left the village, crossing the brook and the valley before climbing up the first hill, they thought of all of the friends they were leaving behind here, but thinking too of all of the friends they would be seeing again at the village of Long River. This time they would not be stopping in the village of Green Stone, so the right turn they made last time Little Star and Gray Eagle had taken this route would not have to be made. A more direct route to Long River would take them in a cold wind direction before turning toward the sunrise direction three or four days from this time. The joy in Brown Fox's heart shone in his face as he led the mother wolf strapped to the travois with the young wolves walking just behind the sides of their mother. Little Star had the chair-seat strapped to her back, but after crossing the brook, White Bear wanted to walk by himself for a time. It wasn't too long and his little legs tired from the pace that Brown Fox, the wolves and Little Star were setting, and he was lifted back into the chair. By midday they had reached the top of the hill, beyond the valley, from where they could see Besh ba Gowah. They turned to see the huts clustered in a big rectangle, the water of the wide brook glistening with the reflection of the trees towering above it. Beyond that was the place of the waterfall and the noisy river down below it. It was a pleasant picture of a vibrant village, one that they would enjoy returning to in the future, the "Great One" willing.

There were two other hills over which they would have to climb before making the right turn, but that was still days ahead. This was still known territory for Little Star, but the excitement of seeing the new land after the turn was always on her mind. Would they be able to find the village of Long River? How long will it take? After making the turn, they came to mountains the tops of which they thought would end near the moon, but no, they were still well below the moon and all of the stars. To find level spots to stop for the nights were a challenge, there was no water to be seen until you walked into shallow springs, and there were no rabbits, turkeys or any visible food sources other than bushes containing leaves and berries. Even the wolves stayed with them in the places they found to stay at. No hunting for them as there was nothing to hunt.

Then, one morning Brown Fox spotted a mountain goat looking out over a very large valley from a ledge in front of them. Brown Fox pointed it out to the male wolf. He "wuffed" quietly and he and the young female wolf stealthily climbed up to the ledge without the goat spotting them. Sensing the approaching danger, the terrified mountain goat lowered its head to try to gore its way out of trouble. The two wolves attacked its forelegs bringing the animal down to its knees, and the male wolf tore its throat from its neck. There would be meat to eat for all of them for a few days. Brown Fox and Little Star took turns scraping the goat's skin from the meat and bones, taking care to keep from tearing any of the main parts such as the sides and over the back bone. Properly dried overnight this would be a good trading item, and the horns could be used for many things as well. The food would be eaten along the way, and that was packaged in small amounts in braided baskets that had been traded for in Besh ba Gowah. This had taken time away from their traveling but furnished them several days of food. They had stayed on the ledge that evening and even set a nice fire to heat the meat they ate. The wolves did not wait to eat heated meat but tore into the pieces that had been torn off for them. From the ledge they could see a faraway village to the sundown direction, a fire blazing, but could not see people there as it was too far away. White Bear had been laid down to sleep and was sleeping soundly. Upon lying down on the sleeping mats, Brown Fox and Little Star gazed up at the moon and stars and together they reached for each other's hands. Little Star said, "What a beautiful evening to be out here with the whole world around us. Would this be a time you want to explore the trail to the moon and stars with me, Brown Fox? "

Brown Fox replied, "Yes, I would like to take the exciting trip with you. As I think back to that first night, I realize what a great privilege you introduced me to, and how good you made me feel. Please don't think badly of me when I say that I hope I can be as pleasurable for you as Gray Eagle was." Little Star answered, "Brown Fox, Gray Eagle and I were best friends from very young on, and knew each other's strengths and weaknesses, likes and dislikes. It takes time to know a person that well, and care for that person that much, to be able to give yourself to that person without question. It may take time for me to know you, and time for you to know me, but we have started to know each other already. Now, enough talk. Help me undress, and I will help you."

The following sun-up they were wakened by strong winds that blew in from the valley below. After a very brief morning snack of leaves and berries, the travois was harnessed to the young male wolf, and they set off walking further back into the woods and then upward, trying to find paths that were wide enough to allow the travois to pass through. It was a zigzagging path they used to get to the very top of the mountain ridge. Judging from the point at which they found themselves, there were several valleys down below that held water. Were any of these waterways part of the long river that led to the village they were seeking? Descending into any of the valleys was going to be a harrowing experience. No easy trails appeared, and for the first time, Brown Fox became alarmed. Little Star came up beside him and gazed down. She, too, was concerned as she saw no route that led to the waterways below. She thought to herself, 'Now is the time to ask the "Great One" for His assistance.'

Raising her hands in front of her, she prayed out loud, "Oh "Great One," please help us find a way to Your life-giving water below. We are lost and searching for the village of Long River. We need Your help, and ask that You furnish a sign for us to follow. Please help us!"

From above came a shrill scream from what sounded like an eagle, and eagle boy swooped down from the sky, and spoke, "Follow me, and I will help you get to the water!" The path that led downward was rocky and steep, but it was passable, and eagle boy guided them down to a point from which a clearer path was seen. The eagle boy made one more pass above them and as softly as a whispered wind, Little Star heard, "The "Great One" heard your prayer for help, and sent me, your son, to help guide you along your path of life. Be not afraid as my duty to the "Great One" is to help in lives of all His creation. You will see me again in the future." With that he soared up and disappeared high into the deep blue sky. A joyful, peaceful feeling came over Little Star as she realized that her son, Flying Eagle, eagle boy, had been sent to help them find their way down the mountainside after her prayer had been said to the "Great One."

It was better than a full two days from the ridge on the top of the mountain to the water down below, but the path to which eagle boy had led them was a lot smoother than the descent that he had directed. That top part took just short of a quarter of sunlight for the day. The bottom path took over a full day and one-half, but they finally reached water. The question then became, "We are here, but where are we?" As Brown Fox peered into the water, he saw that the current was running from left to right, which meant to him that the source of the water would take him closer to finding Long River. He knew there were many waterways that led off of the long river, but by following this current toward the source could mean finding the village of Long River. He explained the theory to Little Star and she agreed that it was a good plan. A day of rest was taken at the side of the water, and a day of playing in the water with White Bear and Brown Fox cleared the thoughts of Little Star. It was fun with the splashing of water between the three travelers, the swinging and dipping White Bear as they had done many nights before. The wolves lay near the water, enjoying the sun and watching their three human friends playing in the water. Little Star was still thinking about eagle boy's rescue of them, and how he had grown into a caring boy with the face of a young Gray Eagle. That was it! He was a part of Gray Eagle, and a part of her! The "Great One" gives, and takes away. Eagle boy, her Flying Eagle, is honored as he will be seen by many, many believers at the will of the "Great One."

Following the water upstream for two days brought them to a branch in the waterway, but they crossed through a shallow part of the branch and continued to walk alongside the main body. This had to be the long river, but where, and how far away was the village of Long River? There was a bend in the river ahead, and Brown Fox recognized it as being an area where the village came to rid the trash, as the current was too strong in which to swim. As they rounded the bend there were shouts of young boys playing alongside the river, and a sigh of relief escaped the mouth of Brown Fox. He had found the village; now to see if anyone remembered him. Were his father and mother still alive? Were Red Wolf and Yellow Moon here? Would he be welcomed as the partner of a traveling trader? The questions swirled around in his head, but he felt as though he was home, and looked forward to meeting with family and friends.

Little Star walked up beside him, looking at the area and the village off to the left of the water line. She turned to Brown Fox, pulled his head down to her lips and kissed him deeply. She said, "Welcome home, Brown Fox. I had faith that you would find it for us. I am so proud of you. You are every bit the man I knew you would be."

As the boys next to the river spotted Brown Fox, Little Star and the three wolves, they shouted out warnings, not knowing who it was, nor what the wolves were doing with the people. It was too far away to see the travois, and these young boys would not have known that traveling traders were beginning to use animals to pull trading goods stacked on travois.

Brown Fox shouted out, "It is me, Brown Fox, a son of the village of Long River. I bring Little Star and her son, White Bear, my partners in the traveling trader business. Little Star is a sister to shaman Red Wolf. Are he and Yellow Moon residents of Long River now?"

Some of the boys came running over to better see the people and the wolves, and remembered the woman to be the traveling trader who long before had visited this village. And, that was Brown Fox with her. He had certainly grown bigger, and he commands the wolves to work for him. He must possess magic, and be an important person. The boys came closer as Brown Fox, Little Star and the wolves advanced alongside the river bank. As they neared the village, people came running out to see what the noise was all about, and seeing the traveling traders approaching, greeted them with the traditional "Ho ah's!" They were returned the "Ho ah's" by Brown Fox and Little Star. Even White Bear blurted out his "Ho ah," which brought out some snickers from the boys surrounding them by this time.

The familiar figure of Red Wolf came down toward the river bank and didn't wait to say his "Ho ah." He walked up to his sister Little Star, gave her a big hug, and walked behind her to look at White Bear. In a very serious tone, he said, "I see you are missing two of your most loved people. I am sure you have had heartache and troubles since we last saw each other. We will talk about that later, but I want to greet you as shaman of the village of Long River. Our chief Two Owls is unable to meet you down here, but will meet you at the special feast in your honor this very evening at the ceremonial pit. Now, let me greet Brown Fox, an honored son of this village. He appears to have grown into a very handsome, strong young man who has control over three, not one, wolves. Brown Fox, I am pleased to see you again. Thank you for bringing my sister to us." Brown Fox replied, "It is an honor to see you as the shaman of Long River, and may I ask about my dear friend, Yellow Moon, your mate? I hear that you now have a daughter named Full Moon. I congratulate you on being her father."

Just then, Yellow Moon came walking up carrying their daughter in her arms. She smiled at Brown Fox and said, "See for yourself, Brown Fox, my dear friend. Our daughter, Full Moon, is far prettier than me. It is so good to see you, and you are looking very handsome and have grown many hands during the past two summers." Turning toward Little Star, she said, "Little Star, welcome to our small part of the world, Long River. I know that you have been here before, as my father and mother talked many times about your promise to ask Red Wolf and me to return to serve this village. Thanks to your persistence, we have done that. It pleases me to see you again." Little Star replied, "It is a pleasure to see you again too, Yellow Moon. We bring both of you greetings from Besh ba Gowah. The distance between the villages is great, but the feelings of peace and harmony exist in both places. The "Great One" has blessed us all."

Brown Fox asked whether the large hut for the use of traveling traders was available, and whether they could all be taken there. Red Wolf replied, "Yes, the hut for visitors is available," and the group resumed walking toward the visitors' hut. Brown Fox had another place he wanted to see after unharnessing the wolf from the travois and unloading the trading goods. He wanted to climb up to see his father and mother who lived in the cave dwellings above the village. As Brown Fox, Red Wolf, Little Star, Yellow Moon, and the villagers were walking toward the hut, an older couple came hurrying from across the river, being carried across by four younger men. As they arrived on the village side, they thanked the carriers and walked up behind the parade that was leading the traders to the hut. Passing the ones in the back as their legs would allow them, they came abreast of the shaman and Yellow Moon. They were noticed by Yellow Moon who said, "Brown Fox, here are your mother and father, Little Mouse and Long Bow."

As Brown Fox turned, the male wolf stopped in its tracks, waiting for Brown Fox to take the next step forward. Instead, Brown Fox walked up to his parents whose eyes misted over as he reached down to grab their hands. He looked from one to the other and told them, "I have come home to see you, bringing with me trading goods of which I am part owner with my partner and best friend, Little Star, and her son, White Bear, whom I consider to be my son as well now."

Surprise showed on the faces of everyone who were within hearing distance as the last part of Brown Fox's words was understood. No one knew what had befallen Little Star's mate, Gray Eagle, but he had apparently walked the path. Also, they did not know that Little Star had birthed twin boys, although Red Wolf and Yellow Moon knew.

Little Star blushed, and thought that she had better explain what had happened to her mate, Gray Eagle, before the people of Long River got the wrong ideas. She asked whether she would be allowed to tell the story of what had happened at the special feast that evening. "It is a tragic story that I prefer to tell just once, rather than many times, because of the hurt and pain that I feel when speaking of it. Would you honor my request, please?"

There were murmurs of agreement heard throughout the gathering crowd. Brown Fox led his father and mother up to the front where the male wolf had waited for him to return to its side before resuming its dragging of the travois to the hut. The female wolves were at the other side of the male wolf as they approached the hut, stopping just beyond the doorway. Brown Fox released the travois from the harness straps and took the harness from the wolf's back. A few of the people near the wolf took a backward step, not trusting that the wolf would not lunge forward and attack them, but there was no sign that would happen. In fact, the male wolf came over next to Brown Fox and licked his leg as if thanking him for relieving it of the burden.

Little Star had been following Brown Fox and the wolves, speaking with her brother Red Wolf and his mate Yellow Moon. She was telling them of the most recent changes at the village of Besh ba Lakado, including how Gray Eagle and Brown Fox had split the lookout's job for the last two winters before Gray Eagle had been killed. She didn't go into any details on that, as she had asked that it be told at the feast that evening. The story of Flying Eagle would be told at that same time, as she could not bring herself to tell the tragic story more than once. However, now that she had seen Flying Eagle and had witnessed some of his duties for the "Great One," she felt that it would not be as bad as before when she had no idea as to why that happened.

The work of unloading the travois and stacking the contents inside the hut was handled by Brown Fox and Little Star. Long Bow helped by standing the travois poles against the back of the hut. Then, Brown Fox offered to take the wolves for a walk around the village to introduce them to the surroundings, asking his father, Long Bow, to accompany him. Little Mouse stayed with Little Star and White Bear, which offered her the opportunity of getting to know the woman who was her son's partner and the young boy whom her son had said he considered to be his son. It was a proud moment for father and son to walk through much of the village, reintroducing Brown Fox to old friends and family. A few of Brown Fox's old friends started asking him about the wolves, and he told them of the attack by the five coyotes on the far side of the mountain of the Thunder God, and how the female wolf single handedly killed the leader of the pack and scattered the rest to protect the camp. And, how the wolves found and brought food for the travelers as they walked from village to village. Yes, the wolves had become an important part of the trading business of which he now was a partner. One of the older boys spoke up and said, "Brown Fox, you are no older than me, and you are a traveling trader, and I am still learning how to make pottery that you buy and sell. You are a very lucky person."

Brown Fox replied, "It has taken much work to learn to become a traveling trader, and nothing is ever given to us as we walk from village to village over many, many days. We own no home, we have everything we own on the top of a travois that is pulled by wild animals we have trained to help us. We treat them with kindness and love, and they work hard for us. We sleep overnight under the great father sky above us with the wind blowing dust, rain and snow in our faces. This is not luck, but hard work."

There were other people who were listening to what Brown Fox had said, and they were proud of this young man who left the safety of this village and took the chance of joining other young people who had dreams just as he had. Long Bow had been unsure of what Brown Fox had wanted to do before he came to him asking his permission to leave the family and join up with the two young traders who were leaving the next morning over three summers ago. It was that he and Little Mouse had three younger children, and six mouths to feed was becoming harder as he grew older. He and Little Mouse had taken a big chance on Brown Fox, allowing him to follow his dream, and look what he had done!

After they had stopped at many of the huts that were occupied by friends or family of Long Bow, Brown Fox wanted to walk over to the big pond where he had first met Gray Eagle, Little Star, and the older female wolf. He remembered being one of the three young boys who had come to this pond to swim and play in the water. Looking across the pond near the tall reeds, they had heard a noise that sounded like a wild animal, and they saw the wolf before they saw the young man and woman standing next to the wolf. How scared he was at first, but then got to know and respect the wolf, and it seemed to take to him too. He thought of the wonderful things that happened, which far outnumbered the bad.

While thinking about some of those things he came to realize that he would have to make a decision on what to tell the people of this village about his relationship with Little Star. He did love her, but was it right? He had loved Yellow Moon too, but that was different. He knew that she was promised to another through her dream catchers which included the "Great One" telling her to leave this village and meet her mate far to the sundown direction near the Thunder God's mountain. She had left the village and he had not seen her again until he entered Besh ba Gowah with Gray Eagle, Little Star and the female wolf. He had never expected to see her again, but she had been there as the mate of Red Wolf, the shaman. He remembered the feeling he had when he first saw her there, and how he longed to go up to her and have her put her arms around him as she had done back here in their own village of Long River.

Now he was a man, a very young man with a huge responsibility. His responsibility as he saw it was to protect Little Star, her son

White Bear, help Little Star and himself be successful in the traveling trader business, and to see as much of the "Great One's" world as he could. He had heard the tales of Kokopelli's travels from the big waters in the sundown direction where huge fish as long as ten men standing on each others' shoulders swam, to the never-ending sands in the sunup direction. He had experienced the heat of the desert, and seen the ice and snow from Long River to Besh ba Lakado. But, was there more? He had to find out. He would ask Little Star if she wanted to go on, or settle down in a village. What would he do if she said she wanted to return to village life rather than continue as a traveling trader? There were dangers to be faced in either place, but the dangers were much higher as a traveling trader. She was willing to risk it before with Gray Eagle and she had consented to come with him and leave Besh ba Lakado. He must ask her what she wants to do, and he must do it soon. All this was going through his mind as he, his father Long Bow, and the wolves were walking back from the pond. His father was telling him about his brother and sister, but he was only listening with one ear. Then, an idea came to him. 'Why not ask the questions that were burning through his mind of a man who has been mated, who has been a father, and who has worked hard to support his family, his own father?'

He asked, "Long Bow, my father, I have some questions to ask you. Would you please help me with these questions that could help me live my life with a more direct purpose?" His father answered, "Yes my son, I will try to answer them as best as I can. What is it you want to know?" Brown Fox began by saying, "I have many responsibilities to my family, to myself, and to those I love. You have these same responsibilities but which one is most important to you?" His father did not hesitate when he replied, "Why that is easy son, all of them are most important. There are ways that you can combine those responsibilities to make them one. You already love and respect family, know yourself well enough that you want to do what you can to protect and care for yourself, and the loves of your life become a part of you. You see son, love is like an ear of corn. You plant a seed, the seed grows and becomes an ear of corn, which you eat. You are caring for that seed from planting to becoming a part of you. That is the same thing as a family; you grow, and the loves of your life become part of you, as your mate and the children you produce together, through the gift of the "Great One." Does that help answer your questions?"

After thinking over what his father told him, he came to the conclusion that he would ask Little Star to become his mate, and they would grow together over time and they would produce children from his seed to her, through the goodness of the "Great One." All she would have to do is say "yes."

While this was going on between Brown Fox and his father, Little Star had laid White Bear down for his nap, something they had no time for while walking toward the village. He was very tired and drifted off to sleep almost immediately. Little Mouse had stayed with Little Star and helped to sort some of the trading goods and prepare the hut for sleeping. Little Mouse noticed that Little Star placed the large sleeping mats together and the smaller one on the side of her own. It was none of her business to ask, but Little Star had a plan in mind to learn more about Brown Fox's family and upbringing. She began, "Little Mouse, I must tell you that my mate walked the path more than one summer ago. We were living at my old home village of Besh ba Lakado on the other side of the Thunder God's mountain more than a moon's walk from here. His name was Gray Eagle, and he and your son Brown Fox split time as the lookout from the caves above the village during the long, hard winter. I will explain tonight at the feast how Gray Eagle walked the path. Gray Eagle and I planned to become traveling traders as I was from the seed of the great traveling trader called Kokopelli, and we listened to many stories he told of visiting villages from the great waters to the unending sands. We grew to long for those places he talked about, and began a trading route shortly after my mother and Kokopelli walked the path. After visiting here, your son, Brown Fox joined us as a partner, and became very good at trading. Gray Eagle and I became father and mother to twin boys, the first is White Bear, the second was called Flying Eagle. Flying Eagle was taken from me in a meadow in front of the lookout's window. A very large eagle came and took my son from the ground near where I was picking flowers. It has been said by many who have seen him that he is the eagle boy who is seen flying above people who have prayed to the "Great One" seeking help. After a summer of mourning my mate's walk and the kidnapping of Flying Eagle, Brown Fox asked whether I wanted to resume the trader's route, and I agreed. I have a great affection for your son, and would ask him to be my mate if you think it would be proper for both him and me. He is like a father to White Bear, and I value his caring and friendship deeply. Do you think it strange that he thinks of White Bear as his son now?"

The answer from Little Mouse was surprising to Little Star. Little Mouse said, "I have prayed to the "Great One" that Brown Fox was safe, and had found a good woman to mate with. The "Great One" made men and women to live together in peace and harmony, creating children through the seed of the man given as a present to the woman. It is good that the "Great One" has favored you with the birth of twins, and even more favored is the mother of the eagle boy. It is said that he shows people the path and takes them to the very gates of the happy hunting grounds. May your life with Brown Fox be blessed with many children, my daughter!"

Little Mouse certainly was straight forward, saying what she thought, and not wasting words. Little Star was sure now that she would be accepted by Brown Fox's mother, and hoped that his father, Long Bow, would have no objections if she were to ask Brown Fox to become her mate. The real approval would have to come from Brown Fox himself, but it would be helpful if both of his parents approved of the mating.

Brown Fox and Long Bow had just come up in front of the hut in which Little Star and Little Mouse were finishing the stacking of the trade goods against the inside walls. The wolves were tethered to the exposed root of an old ironwood tree next to the hut, and then the men entered the hut. Seeing the sleeping mats laying on the floor with the two large mats together and the smaller with White Bear sleeping to the side, a smile crossed the face of Long Bow, and he gave a quick glance to Brown Fox. He thought to himself, 'perhaps Little Mouse has spoken to Little Star about mating with Brown Fox and set up the sleeping mats herself. She has prayed long and hard to the "Great One" to protect Brown Fox and to provide him with a good mate. Little Mouse looks very pleased, so that must be the reason.' Brown Fox was a bit confused to see the sleeping mats lain out already, but secretly was pleased that his father and mother would be aware of the close quarters that Little Star and he had to share while traveling. At least his father knew of his feelings toward Little Star, and would be able to convince Little Mouse that they could be mated soon, that is if she would accept his proposal.

White Bear woke up as Brown Fox and Long Bow had brushed the curtain at the doorway just to let Little Star and Little Mouse know that they were entering. He sat up looking at the two new people standing inside the hut, and asked, "Momma, who are these people?" Little Star replied, "This is Long Bow, a hunter for the village of Long River and father of Brown Fox. And, this is Little Mouse, mate of Long Bow and mother of Brown Fox. It is good for us to meet them, and we will be seeing them several times while we stay here in this village. We will visit them in their home up in the cave across the river after our trading day is done tomorrow, if that would be acceptable to them."

Little Mouse was overjoyed to hear that they would be willing to come up to their home inside the cave that overlooked the river and village. She volunteered the invitation, "White Bear, we would be honored if you, your mother Little Star and Brown Fox would come for a visit tomorrow after the trading is done. In fact, we would be honored if you spent the day with us while your mother and Brown Fox do their trading."

Little Star spoke up immediately saying, "I don't approve of him leaving us. I have lost one son already, and do not want to lose the other. Please allow us to bring him with us after the trading is done tomorrow. I am sorry, but I just can't let him go without Brown Fox or me."

The sound of a bell rang out as one of the young girls of the village walked through the area, signaling the gathering for the evening meal which was being readied at the ceremonial pit. Little Star remembered giving that bell, which was given to her in Besh ba Gowah, to Singing Water the first time they had met in Long River. Brown Fox picked up White Bear, took the hand of Little Star and ushered his father and mother, Long Bow and Little Mouse, out of the doorway ahead of them. Placing White Bear behind his head with his short little legs around his neck, all five of them strode down toward the pottery jars of water that were at the entrance to the ceremonial pit. These were freshly poured jars of water used for washing hands and faces before sitting down to eat. There were three circles of varying height with the center circle reserved for the chief, his mate, the shaman and his family, and the people for whom the feast was being held. An old man recognized by Brown Fox and Little Star as being chief Two Owls, an old woman who was his mate, Singing Water, were seated with their backs to the sundown direction. Red Wolf the shaman, Yellow Moon, and Full Moon, his mate and daughter, were seated across from the chief and Singing Water. Brown Fox, Little Star and White Bear were seated with their backs to the hot winds direction with the other two seats for Brown Fox's parents, Long Bow and Little Mouse. A second circle was for the elders of the village, while the third was for the younger members, cooks and serving people.

After the seating had been completed, Red Wolf stood and gave a blessing prayer. "We thank you "Great One" for returning Brown Fox to our village, and bringing my sister, Little Star and her son White Bear, for the purpose of trading with us. We look forward to hearing of their lives as traveling traders and hope that their stay with us, however long that might be, will provide all of us with the love, peace and harmony we seek in our lives." He sat down and the food was served to the people in the inner circle, then the other two circles.

Conversations took place between the people in each of the circles, but most of the people were waiting for the explanation of Little Star as to the absence of Gray Eagle, and the twin child they had heard so much about from shaman Red Wolf and his mate Yellow Moon.

The food was served on large wooden platters with turkey being the meat. Squash, beans, watercress and blackberries were served along with a sweet drink tasting like honey water. It was the best meal the traveling traders had tasted since leaving Besh ba Gowah, and they ate hungrily. After the meal had been eaten, two men came over behind and to the side of chief Two Owls, helping him to rise and supporting him as he stood. In a halting and shallow voice he announced. "It is a great honor to have Brown Fox return to us, his home village of Long River. He has seen and done many things of honor and I would invite him to stand and tell us of some of his travels and work."

Brown Fox stood and began to speak in a voice that could be heard easily in the back circle. "I am honored to return to Long River, my home village and tell you that I have seen and done many things of note. Having left to join Little Star and her mate, Gray Eagle, was a dream come true for me. They accepted me as a partner. I helped with the work that traveling traders must do like packing, carrying, loading and unloading of trade goods. We set up camps under the "Great One's" skies, and traveled great distances to villages in the desert, mountains and valleys, and stayed for two winters at the faraway village of Besh ba Lakado, the home village for our shaman, Red Wolf, and his sister, Little Star. My story has been told, but hers is more important to hear, as it concerns her former mate, Gray Eagle and her second born twin son, Flying Eagle. I ask that she tell you her story now." Then, he sat down encouraging Little Star to stand and speak.

Little Star began, "As my mate Gray Eagle and I left the village of Long River, Brown Fox began following us. During the first night, he joined us, telling us he had permission from his father and mother, Long Bow and Little Mouse, if we would accept him. He has been a huge help to us during the time he has been a partner in the trading business. We visited the village of Large House, meeting Pretty Sky, Brave Beaver's mate in the fields outside the village. She escorted us past the armed guards and into the square in front of the big house occupied by chief Black Coyote, who would not let us get closer than the doorway of his big house. He requested a present before allowing us to set up our own trading platform the following day, not offering a meal to us, nor to the women and children of the village. There were no men to be seen in the entire village. The trading was very poor as none of the villagers owned anything of value, not even coverings for their feet. We left what we could for the villagers' use, and departed early the next sun-up. We next traveled to Besh ba Gowah, where the "Great One" allowed me to birth twin boys, the first being White Bear who sits with us here, the second was named Flying Eagle. After taking time for me to rest after giving birth, we traveled to Gray Eagle's and my home village of Besh ba Lakado, behind the Thunder God's mountain. As we rested the night before arriving at the village, five coyotes tried attacking us, and the female wolf defended us by killing the leader and putting the rest to flight. A male wolf joined us, and the young wolves with us now were the result of their mating. We arrived at Besh ba Lakado just before the first snowfall, and since the lookout had walked the path, we were asked if Gray Eagle would accept being the lookout from the cave above the village while we stayed there. It was a perfect place for us to live as Gray Eagle's father and mother lived there, too. They were the heads of the hunters and gatherers, and were in charge of the supply rooms for the cave dwellers. Our home was on the very edge of the cave, looking out over the village, lake and valley below. Because of their keen eyesight, Gray Eagle and Brown Fox split time at the spirit window, allowing the other to accompany the hunters, and taking the wolves with them while they were around. The wolves did hunting on their own before the female birthed the two pups.

"While watching from above, Gray Eagle saw a ledge above the end of the lake in the mountain to the sunup direction that he wanted to visit in the early spring. From that ledge, he would be able to see the entire lake, valley and village and the mountains that protected them. He left early one morning, taking the male wolf with him. We watched as he passed the village, following the shoreline of the lake to the forest of trees leading upward into the mountain that contained the ledge. He had taken two of the birds that flew between us with him, and the first one returned just before sundown the first night. He had thought that it would take him the second day to climb up to the ledge, and planned to light a fire up on the ledge to let us know when he arrived there."

She choked back a sob and continued. "No fire was lit the next night, and we waited another full day, but no fire was ever seen. I sent for Gray Eagle's father, Straight Arrow, head of the hunters for the village, asking him to head a search party to find Gray Eagle. The group left early the next sunup, following the path that Gray Eagle had taken. Near sundown the second day, from the spirit window, Brown Fox saw the group emerge onto the ledge holding the wrapped straight body of Gray Eagle, laying it on the ledge for it to watch over the area for all time. Upon the group's return, we were told that Gray Eagle had been attacked by a cougar and killed. Straight Arrow and the group with him killed the cougar. They found the cage with the bird dead inside, but were unable to find the male wolf. It was found dead later in a tree trap set by our hunters during the previous winter. I mourned for much time before being able to face the world again. Through the support of Gray Eagle's mother and father, Brown Fox's understanding, the comfort of taking care of my two sons, and a dream catcher in which Gray Eagle returned to me telling me that he would be with me forever through our sons, it allowed me to live again." Her sobs started again as she said; "I took my two sons out to a meadow beneath the spirit window one day, and as I was bending over to pick some flowers, the largest eagle I have ever seen dove down, picked up my son, Flying Eagle, and flew off over the lake and the mountains beyond. I have heard that many people have seen eagle boy since that time, but I had not seen him until a few days ago as Brown Fox, White Bear, the wolves and I became lost in the mountains in the sundown direction from here. In despair, I prayed to the "Great One" for help, and eagle boy, my son, Flying Eagle, flew down and guided us through a trail that could not be seen from where we had been trapped. Eagle boy's face has become that of a young Gray Eagle, and I was so happy to see it again. I really can't go on, so please excuse me. I must take White Bear and return to the hut to reflect on what I have told you."

With that, Little Star rose, picked up White Bear and departed the circles with tears streaming down her face. Brown Fox got up, bowed to the people in the first circle and followed in Little Star's footsteps, saying, "Please excuse me, I must try to help, if I can."

He caught up to Little Star, putting his arm around her shoulders and walking beside her to the doorway of the hut. He could not think of words to say that would help, but just the arm around her comforted and let her know she was not alone in her grief. After entering the hut, Little Star gave White Bear a kiss on his cheek and lay him down on his sleeping pad. She said, "Go to sleep my little man, and we will see each other in the sunlight of tomorrow." Turning to sit down on her sleeping mat, she sat with her face in her hands, still weeping. Brown Fox went over to the side of the hut where a small pottery crock held some drinking water. He poured some into a wooden cup, brought it to her, and sat down on his sleeping mat next to her. In a few moments, she raised her head, and seeing the water being offered, she took it from his hands, thanked him, and took a swallow. Handing it back to Brown Fox, she looked into his eyes and said, "I am sorry for the words I said, and the feelings I had while speaking about my personal tragedies. I want you to know that I love you and respect you, not only for the work you do, and the love you show to White Bear, me and the wolves, but because you are a good man. I invite you to become a part of me at any time you want to fill my heart and body with your goodness. I ask you to be my mate, and promise to honor you as long as I live."

Brown Fox was stunned by the offer, as he had planned to make the offer to her. It took but a moment for him to answer, saying, "Little Star, you have made my dream catcher come true. I have thought about asking you to become my mate, and now I find that you have asked me. I promise to be the best I can be for you." With that, they embraced and slowly lay down together on her mat. A wonderful trip to the moon and stars lasted a long time as waves of love passed between the two of them.

The next sunup a pulse of excitement rushed through the village. The traveling traders were setting up their wares on the benches that had been brought into the trading area, and as they passed some of the huts to arrive there, the residents of several huts watched for items they may need or want as the travois passed by their doorways. The trading began with many flint items being requested as the limestone this village was built on did not have good flint nearby. In exchange, many reeds, baskets, blankets, footwear and hides of animals were accepted by Brown Fox and Little Star. There were pottery and intricate jewelry pieces that were exchanged for seeds of cotton plants, knapped arrow and spear points, and heavy woven cotton clothing for the cold winters. Some of the items offered by the villagers were too large, or too heavy to transport, and had to be turned down as trades. Snowshoes and skis were not tradable as Brown Fox, Little Star and White Bear would be walking back into the hot deserts below, where those items were not required. All in all, the trading went smoothly, and many of the villagers returned for other items they desired but could not initially acquire for lack of value on their side of the trade. Their second visit brought finer items that were then traded for the more valuable items Brown Fox and Little Star had to offer.

As the sun reached the half-way distance between midday and the trees next to the path leading to the river below, trading was ended for the day, and Brown Fox brought the travois over to be loaded, and then strapped to the young female wolf. Loading did not take too long as the items Little Star and Brown Fox had received were lighter than the items they had brought into Long River. White Bear had been playing with the wolves which had been tethered to one of the stumps that made up the end of the display area, and was unhappy when the young wolf was led away to be harnessed. It was funny to hear him snort and grunt much like the wolves did when communicating with each other. It occurred to Brown Fox that White Bear may be learning the language of the wolf along with learning the human language. White Bear did use some words that he had heard over and over, but he had not put sentences together yet. That would come soon, as Brown Fox promised himself he would begin working with him on communicating. It was still daylight when they left the trading area, arrived at the hut, and unloaded the travois. They hurried to get ready to cross the river and climb up to Long Bow and Little Mouse's cave dwelling, hoping to stay there for a time getting to know Brown Fox's family before returning to the hut in which they were staying in the village.

Crossing the river was not too hard as there were thick, flat stepping stones placed in easily seen places, and were spaced so that even children could cross using them. The path up to the cave was well marked and not too steep. As they approached the entrance to the cave they were met by Long Bow, who escorted them to the family hut. Everyone enjoyed the time, conversation, and evening meal spent together high above the village of Long River, which reminded Little Star of the time Gray Eagle, Brown Fox, White Bear, Flying Eagle and she had spent in the look-out's home above Besh ba Lakado. Rather than the large lake they had seen at Besh ba Lakado, this offered a beautiful view of the river, the village of Long River, and a large forest of scrub pine trees that seemed to stretch for a day's travel. As the sun began its descent behind the mountains to the sundown direction, Brown Fox, Little Star and White Bear began their trip back down to the river crossing, and to their hut inside the village. It had been a full day, and it was dark by the time they reached the hut. A comfortable and restful night was enjoyed by Brown Fox, Little Star and White Bear.

The following day offered a second day of trading, and brought out the first buffalo blanket Little Star had ever seen. One of the hunters where Long Bow and Little Mouse lived had been on what he called a long trip toward the early sunrise direction, and had killed one of the huge shaggy beasts he called a buffalo. The blanket was very large, thick and warm, but it was not offered for trade. The hunter brought it down to show the traveling traders his prized possession. Little Star exclaimed; "That is the largest blanket I have ever seen! It must have been a giant animal. It has been said by my mother in one of my dream catchers that my son, White Bear, will become a great hunter of these huge shaggy animals you call buffalo. He is still young now, but he will get bigger and stronger, and will find these buffalo and kill them to feed and clothe many people. My mother is a spirit, and cannot lie."

Shaman Red Wolf came over to their trading area to invite Brown Fox, Little Star and White Bear to share evening meal with Yellow Moon, Full Moon and him. They would have much to talk about, and the meal was a short part of the evening. Little Star asked her brother, Red Wolf, "Do you think it proper for a woman to ask a man to be her mate, or do you think that it should be the man to ask the woman?" Red Wolf smiled and answered, "Does it matter if they both feel the same way about each other? I do expect there may be more than that question that bothers you, Little Star. Do you have someone in mind, and might he know of your interest and concern? Perhaps he may feel the same way about you. Do you have the same feelings about Little Star, Brown Fox?" The question came so fast that Brown Fox was stunned temporarily. He stammered, "How, how did you know, Red Wolf?" Red Wolf and Yellow Moon both laughed, and Yellow Moon answered for the two of them, saying, "We could see it in your eyes when your eyes met, and see the caring you have for each other as you left the feast last night. You are both young enough to share many moons and stars together, and bring many children into the world." Shaman Red Wolf smiled as he said, "Little Star, I wouldn't wait too long to mate with Brown Fox. You would not want to let him get away, would you?" They all laughed at the words of Red Wolf, and Little Star said, "I had better ask him now then, shouldn't I? Brown Fox, will you be my mate?" This time Brown Fox was ready for the question and smiling broadly, said, "I thought you would never ask. Red Wolf, when would be a convenient time for you to perform the mating ceremony?" Red Wolf replied, "Would tomorrow just before sundown be too early?"

Word spread throughout the village the next day that a mating ceremony for Brown Fox and Little Star would take place after the evening meal at the ceremonial pit. Many of the villagers spent time readying themselves for the mating ceremony. Chief Two Owls, his mate Singing Water, Long Bow, Little Mouse and their three children, Yellow Moon and Full Moon, Red Wolf's mate and daughter, and White Bear made up the center circle with Brown Fox and Little Star standing in front of shaman Red Wolf. The second circle still contained many of the elders of the clan, but only a few of the young people remained to attend the ceremony. The pottery mating vase with two spouts and a double-pointed stick of about two hands long were brought to Red Wolf. The stick had been painted half blue and half red with berry juices. As Brown Fox and Little Star stood hand-in-hand, the shaman scratched the upper arm of both with the sharpened points-the right arm of Brown Fox, the left of Little Star-bringing forth just a trickle of blood from both. Guiding the arms of both Brown Fox and Little Star to where the blood of each touched, Red Wolf announced, "Brown Fox and Little Star, you are now one." Breaking the stick in half and putting an end into each of the two spouts, he dropped the vase into the fire below, breaking the vase. This signified that the mating would last until the two walked the path to the happy hunting grounds.

A flute player and a drummer began the slow beat of a dance, rising in tempo and sound as the members of the clan stood up and began to move to the cadence of the music, making their movements resemble the coupling of man and woman visiting the moon and stars together. After a short while of watching the dancers, Brown Fox and Little Star took White Bear by the hand and hurried back to the hut in which they would spend the night soaring beyond the moon and searching out many stars.

After staying at the village of Long River for a total of five days, Brown Fox and Little Star decided it was time to leave. They had enjoyed seeing Red Wolf, Yellow Moon and their daughter Full Moon. Brown Fox and Little Star had hopes of returning to Long River again someday, and hoped to see them at that later visit. It would be the last time they would see chief Two Owls and his mate Singing Water, as they were getting old and would be walking the path soon, of that they were sad. Brown Fox had seen his father, mother, two brothers and a sister, and he hoped that they would have more time together before they would walk the path. His brothers were now ten and nine summers, his sister seven, so they may see them when they returned here. The rest of Brown Fox's family and friends were sorry to see them leave, but they had to get back to work as traveling traders.

The travois was loaded, and early the next morning the male wolf was harnessed, the poles inserted, the straps tightened, and they began their walk, retracing their steps toward Besh ba Gowah, by way of the village of Green Stone.

CHAPTER 6

The mostly level walk toward the hot winds direction was much easier on the feet, knees and legs of the walkers, and even the wolves seemed to appreciate the level dragging of the travois. The route followed the long river from which the village got its name. The first day they walked much farther than they had when approaching the village of Long River from a slightly different direction. After three days they turned to the sundown direction where they encountered a number of mountains and valleys that would slow them, dry them out and quickly tire their bodies. They did not have to go as far to the hot wind direction as when they were going to the village of Large House, but the terrain was much more difficult to travel. They found springs and waterways in the green valleys between the mountains, but they never knew where to find them until they almost stepped into them. They had received traveling foods from the residents of Long River, but not enough to last the many days it would take to get to Green Stone. The leaves from bushes, berries, and a beehive that was full of honey were helpful in keeping the group alive and forcing them to walk onward. Day after day they would climb up and then look for a safe way to go down the mountains, and the valleys were always short with much vegetation to walk around. Finally, after seven days of the mountains, they arrived at an area that joined up with a river. It had been said that the long river that flowed past the village of Long River flowed all the way to the big waters, but no one had ever followed it that far. It appeared to have gone around the mountains over which Brown Fox had led Little Star, White Bear, and the wolves, but they could not see where it even appeared at the end of the faraway mountains to the hot winds direction. And, there was no proof that this was the same river.

As they crested a hill, looking toward the sundown direction, they saw what looked like smoke rising in the distance. It would be right for the evening meal to be prepared, and they hoped the fire originated in the village of Green Stone. While Little Star went down to the river bank to bring water for their cooking pot, Brown Fox unharnessed the young female wolf from the travois, then began to make a circular camp with the limbs of some fallen branches of trees in the area. A few of the dried out twigs were enough to start a small fire with the use of flints, and larger thin branches were added as the fire took. Little Star had found two bird eggs in a nest alongside the bank, and the male wolf brought over a quail it had caught running under a willow tree that leaned over the river bank, but had a few branches fanned out on this side. The quail was fat and juicy, just enough to give Brown Fox, Little Star and White Bear a small piece of the quail's breast, and the two eggs were split between the three of them. There were berries that had been picked as they walked along the bank of the river that whole day, and those became a satisfying addition to the meal and sweetened the water drink they had poured. As the darkness covered their campsite, they saw a fire off in the direction of the smoke they had seen earlier. It did appear to be a village, not a mobile band of hunters, gatherers, or raiders. Little Star had taken pains to keep their fire low, partially hidden by a small hill that would protect the fire from being seen by anyone from the sundown side, where the other fire was seen. The next morning they would take their time to wash themselves in the river, eat a small meal of leaves, berries and water before walking toward what they hoped was the village of Green Stone.

A half-day of walking brought them to a small hill from which they could see into the village ahead. It appeared to be Green Stone, but there was little movement taking place within the village. The fields that were growing crops of corn, squash, beans, and cotton were not flourishing as they should be at this time of year. The water level in the canals leading to the furrows was down to where it was a trickle, not at all the amount of water needed for the crops to grow strongly. A small hill had formed and pushed the river flow from the canal mouth around to the hot wind side behind and beyond the village. Brown Fox and Little Star saw several men of the village feverishly trying to dig deeper canals to bring the water flow back to the fields that needed the water so badly. The women were out with baskets filled with dirt that had been removed, dragging them around and trying to build a wall to reroute the flow of water. It was evident that both men and women were failing in their efforts.

Brown Fox called out to the women who were closest to him as they approached the village, saying, "People of Green Stone, we are traveling traders, Brown Fox, Little Star, our son, White Bear, and three wolves who are our friends and work with us. We see what you are trying to do, and want to help if we can." One of the women stopped dragging her loaded basket, wiped her forehead and said, "The hill began growing and changed the direction of the water flow after we had planted our crops. We have been taking turns trying to reroute the flow of water one day, and carrying water from the river the next. The water we haul is never enough for the crops to grow well, and the digging and dragging the dirt to build a wall to redirect the flow has not helped either. We have no more seeds to plant new fields next to the river, so it is do what we can to save what we can grow, or starve. Our hunters and gatherers have been out for two days now, but have not returned with anything more than a few quail, a small turkey, and berries. Leaves would now taste good to those of us still in the village if we could find some that are edible.

Do you have any food or seeds we can trade for? That would be the biggest help you could offer us." Brown Fox replied, "We have seeds for corn, beans, squash, and cotton. We could offer you help in planting the seeds if your men will dig the canals near where the river bends. As for the hill that is growing, what makes it grow?" The woman answered, "If we knew that we would be able to know how to stop it. There is a noise that sounds like thunder, and a hissing sound that comes from within the hill. We are afraid of it, but we can't leave without food, and all of our possessions would be impossible to move quickly."

Little Star had come up close enough to have heard the woman's reply, and asked, "Has Gray Cougar, your shaman, called on the "Great One" to help?" The woman, who was now walking toward the approaching traveling trader group, answered, "He has been praying for the past seven days, but no answers have come to him yet. I recognize you, but the man who is with you now is not the man who was with you the last time you visited our village. At that time you did not have a son and had only one wolf with you. Why do you travel with wolves, and don't they hurt you? It has been over three summers since your last visit. You and your mate were good traders for our village back then. Will you help us this time, too?" Little Star replied, "We will do what we can to help. Do you still have the hut set aside for visitors in the village? We are tired from our long journey, and would appreciate resting for awhile before we begin to help. We will explain our travels later."

The woman called out to another of the women who was still dragging a basket filled with dirt saying, "Little Sparrow, I am taking these traveling traders into the village to the visitors' hut. As you can see, the woman is Little Star, one of the traders that visited three summers ago. I will return after taking them to the hut." With that said, she led the group toward the village. The two young wolves were at Brown Fox's side as he held a woven reed rope that was attached to the older female wolf that was pulling the travois. Little Star was carrying White Bear in the sitting chair on her back. As they entered the village, some of the elders of the village, and a few children began shouting that there were wild animals entering the village, which brought out more people into the main part of the village.

A large man dressed in a prayer robe stepped out of the largest hut near the back of the village, and Little Star recognized Gray Cougar, the shaman who had looked into her eyes and told her that she would deliver twins. Their eyes met, and a great, peaceful smile appeared on his lips as he came forward to greet her. However, she spoke first, saying, "Ho ah, shaman Gray Cougar! It is me, Little Star. I greet you and it becomes my honor to tell you that you were correct when you told me that I would deliver twin sons. They were born in the village of Besh ba Gowah. But, the "Great One" gives and takes away. This is my first born son, White Bear, but the second born was taken by a giant eagle and put into the service of the "Great One." He is now known as eagle boy, whose job it is to help those who pray for help to the "Great One." Gray Eagle was taken from me by the attack of a cougar, and this is my new mate and partner of whom I am very proud. His name is Brown Fox."

Gray Cougar answered, "Ho ah, Little Star! It is a great pleasure to see you again, and to meet Brown Fox and your son, White Bear. A dream catcher I had the night before last told me that we would meet again soon, and that your arrival would be of great help to this village. You have one man and one son with you, but I am unsure if the three of you can provide the help we need. I have been praying to the "Great One" for seven days and seven nights, but so far nothing has changed in our quest to produce better food crops. The hill that changed the course of the water from the mouth of the canals to flow around and behind the village has continued to grow. There is not enough food to offer you a meal of celebration on your arrival, but perhaps we can fill your bodies with berries and water until we find a solution to this problem. Allow me to lead you to the visitors' hut." The woman who had been leading the group into the village left to return to the basket that she was pulling before, and resumed her work.

Arriving at the hut, Brown Fox loosened the travois poles from the harness and took the harness from the female wolf's back. As he did so, the people surrounding the shaman and the traveling traders took a step back, not knowing if the wolf would attack them. It was funny to watch their amazement when the wolf went to the side of Brown Fox rubbing his leg with its side fur. The two young wolves came over to their mother and licked the sides of its face. This was startling behavior for wild animals. The people marveled at how well they were trained.

Little Star had been talking with shaman Gray Cougar as they were walking to the hut, telling him about Gray Eagle's death and the eagle taking Flying Eagle from the meadow, flying over the lake and beyond the mountains across the valley. Since she had been telling a shaman the events, she was better able to control her feelings, although the growing number of villagers following them began 'oohing' and 'ahhing' as the story unfolded. Little Star felt comfortable with Gray Cougar because of his foretelling of her delivering the twin sons three summers past. She had gone to him feeling uncomfortable and knowing that she was with child. She had asked for something to relieve her discomfort, but he had just looked into her eyes and said to her, "Little Star, I see the discomfort comes not from your body, but from your mind. I see you are blessed and you will birth twin boys." This happened just as Gray Cougar had told her. He had also said that many people would be helped by her, her mate, their children and the many animals who would consider her their mother because of her caring for them. She felt blessed for having met this holy man the first time, and felt the same way following this brief meeting.

After the travois was unloaded and the contents stacked within the hut, the poles were stored behind the hut. Little Star took White Bear inside and laid him down on his sleeping mat to take a nap, then laid down on hers. She had been thinking about the situation the village of Green Stone was facing and prayed to the "Great One" in hopes of coming up with a solution to their problem. What had made the hill grow near the opening to the vital canal that watered the fields? What were the sounds that came from beneath the hill? Is there a way to dig down to find the source, or was it too dangerous to do that? What must occur for the water to be rerouted to the fields, at least for this growing season? The villagers could plant fields nearer the river next season if the food and seeds produced this year could be harvested. She knew that Brown Fox and she had some seeds in their trading goods that could be used here, but nowhere near the number that would be required to replace the ones already planted and dying in the fields for lack of water. If only it would rain! It would have to be a good rain, not hard, but a slow, steady rain for a good part of the day. That would help for a time, but would not solve the problem permanently. Slowly she drifted off to sleep, thinking about the crops wilting away in the fields with the water so close, yet so faraway.

Brown Fox had taken the wolves out to the bend in the river for them to drink, and he was bringing some water back for Little Star, White Bear and himself for later that evening. As he was returning, he saw the hill that had been growing near the entrance to the canal leading to the growing fields. A tree that had been growing on the level ground before the hill started pushing up was bent and gnarled. The tree was located at the very point from which the hill curved upward to knee height, and the hill extended about the length of four people standing on each other's shoulders. It was tall enough to divert the water flow from the canal leading to the growing fields. He decided to take a closer look at that tree and the area around it. There was a twisted root extending from a hole under the tree with a small amount of white silt being pushed out from under the tree. Brown Fox had lived in the cave dwellings across and above the river at the village of Long River, and had seen trees growing along the river with the same white silt being pushed up by the surging water below. He thought to himself, 'There is a spring below pushing the silt upward and out this hole. Maybe it would be best to enlarge the hole and allow the water to flow from there, which may relieve the pressure below and collapse the hill.'

He hurried to the hut, woke up Little Star and began explaining his idea to her. She became excited when she heard Brown Fox's idea, woke and picked up White Bear, and the three of them rushed over to see shaman Gray Cougar. After hearing the explanation, Brown Fox led Gray Cougar, Little Star and White Bear over to see the tree and white silt, and then the four went to see chief Big Bear at the chief's hut.

After brushing the curtain at the doorway of the chief's hut, the chief's grandson, Brown Bear came and invited them to enter. Brown Bear had been sitting with Big Bear listening as his grandfather explained an important decision that he had made about distributing the remaining food to the villagers. Big Bear remained sitting but asked the visitors to sit in a circle facing the center, with Brown Bear sitting next to his grandfather. Brown Fox, Little Star and Gray Cougar exchanged greetings with the chief and Brown Bear, and shaman Gray Cougar excitedly announced that Brown Fox had an idea that may help collapse the hill and redirect the water flow back to the canal. The shaman asked Brown Fox to explain the idea which he did. This was recognized as an idea that was different, but it had to be tried to see if it would work. The group then talked about how the digging could be done to promote the silt to move more freely, and release the hoped-for water to create a new path. Digging a channel back to the entrance of the canal leading to the fields would not be hard as the flow of water would soften the soil. The shaman said a prayer that the effort would be blessed and successful, and the group prepared to leave. The chief stood up, bowed to Brown Fox, and said, "You are a gifted thinker for one so young. Thank you for your idea. If this works to refresh our fields, you will receive a gift of my finest jeweled bracelet," showing it fastened to his left wrist. After that, the group left the chief's hut and walked back through the village.

Brown Fox took White Bear in his arms, carried him to the hut and placed him sitting up on his sleeping mat. Next, he took out some leaves, berries and poured water into wooden mugs he took from one of the trading packs for their evening meal. He had noticed that White Bear was getting bigger and stronger, and he would not be getting carried much anymore. White Bear was beginning to talk in short sentences, and was asking many questions about visiting different villages, and why he couldn't stay at one to play with some of the friends he was beginning to make. Yes, he was growing up and would need to be taught the things that boys needed to know. He was getting to be at an age where he could begin doing small tasks like gathering twigs for starting a fire, stretching out the sleeping mats, taking water to the birds in their cages, and walking the wolves for exercise when they were within a village. Brown Fox knew that he must be a big part of the teaching process, and he looked forward to it.

Little Star was very proud of Brown Fox's idea, and as they walked side-by-side, said to shaman Gray Cougar, "Brown Fox has been a real blessing to me, and I value his courage, determination and his strong mind. We have been mates for such a short time, but friends for just over three years. I find out things about him every day as we travel paths that are not known to us. He watches for the colors of the leaves on trees to indicate water, moss grown on the sides of trees to indicate the directions, has been good at guiding and caring for the wolves, loves my son as his own, and is very good at determining the worth of a trade." Shaman Gray Cougar turned and said to Little Star, "He is good at planting his seed, too. Although it is very early in its life, I see that you will birth another child, this time a daughter. You will have about seven moons to prepare for her. Be very careful, as this daughter will have a very difficult and short life. This is all I can tell you."

Little Star was surprised, as she thought that her flow was just late this moon. As he finished speaking, they were arriving at the shaman's hut. He turned toward her, taking her small hands in his big ones, and saying, "We will begin the process of digging in the hill tomorrow at sunrise. I am afraid that the trading you were expecting to do here will be very unsuccessful. The residents of Green Stone are trying to keep everything they can in order to stay alive. We must find a way to water the fields and bring the crops back to life so that we may continue to live. Without food, we will all wither and die, becoming like the blowing, dry soil. Thank you for your friendship and the wisdom brought to this village by your mate Brown Fox. We will see each other after sunrise." With that, he turned and entered his hut.

Little Star walked to the hut in which Brown Fox and White Bear had finished eating their leaves and berries, and were drinking the water from the wooden mugs. There were leaves and berries set aside for Little Star, and Brown Fox poured water for her to drink. Little Star looked over at Brown Fox and said, "Brown Fox, I can't begin to tell you how proud of you I am. Your idea may save this entire village from starvation. We must pray together that the digging will result in the hoped-for water below to create a new path to the canal. It will probably take a few days for the digging to be completed, but I believe that the sound we hear from under the hill is the water pushing its way up from below."

Brown Fox agreed that a prayer to the "Great One" would be a wonderful request for this village to receive help in staying alive. They prayed together, and then took to their sleeping mats. White Bear fell asleep quickly, with Brown Fox following in short order. Little Star lay awake, thinking of what she had been told by shaman Gray Cougar. "He is good at planting his seed, too. Although it is very early in its life, I see that you will birth another child, this time a daughter. You will have seven moons to prepare for her. Be very careful, as this daughter will have a very difficult and short life." This was a worrisome thing to hear. Seven moons to prepare! Where would they be in seven moons? She knew they would be going back to Besh ba Gowah, as it was on the way as they headed toward the sundown direction. Brown Fox and she had talked about traveling to the great waters, but that was many, many moons from here, or even from Besh ba Lakado. Did this mean they would have to stop their traveling trader route before they actually got started? These were questions only time would answer, but the worries began to cloud her mind that evening. Many of her dream catchers that night were kept for her to see at daylight, as some of the bad dreams remained, and she was frightened for herself and her unborn baby.

The next morning the sky in the sunup direction showed a multitude of colors reflecting off high clouds, none of which indicated rain. As the sun peeked over the horizon, the birds near the river were chirping loudly. The wolves were over getting drinks, and had spotted a turkey that had wandered in from a wooded area the travelers had passed by the day before. It had no defense against the three wolves, which awarded the prize to the mother wolf which brought it directly to the hut of Brown Fox and Little Star, dropping it just outside the curtain. The wolves stood protecting it as some of the villagers had spotted them bringing it through the village. As hungry as the villagers were, they did not want to try to take it from the animals. The male wolf brushed its tail against the door covering, and Brown Fox sprang to his feet to see what was happening. Seeing the wolves, the dead turkey, and the residents hungrily watching every move the wolves were making, he pushed the thin curtain to the side, walked out, and asked that the head cook of the village come over to help prepare the turkey for a mid-day meal. The assembled villagers gave a cheer, as now they knew they would have some meat for a change, not a lot, but at least a taste of something besides leaves and berries.

Chief Big Bear had been told of the offer of food to the village, and came over to thank Brown Fox. He also gave the order to begin digging near the exposed root of the gnarled tree on the side of the growing hill, and some of the men began to walk over to see the hole of which Brown Fox had spoken to the chief and shaman. Nobody had gone over to see the old tree before this. Just as the fields were wilting, the tree had not been deeply rooted and was not getting any water. Thinking that it could be used for firewood after dying, it was left for its future use. These people had lived in this village for a very long time, and had not faced a problem as severe as this ever during their lives. Their hunters had grown fat and lazy, unable and unwilling to make the long treks into the wooded areas that would harbor the deer, javelinas, quail, turkeys, or other meaty animals. After all, they would then have to carry the meat and hides all the way back to the village. It was easier to plant the crops, watch them grow and harvest them when that work had to be done. This situation led to a necessary change in living and working habits, and they were re-discovering the needs they had taken for granted for so long. Perhaps it was not too late to seek a good life which would include work.

Little Star woke to hear the talking outside the curtain, turned over to look at the back of Brown Fox and the crowd of people facing him and the wolves. She heard the sound of Big Bear's voice and heard the thank you he had spoken to Brown Fox. She was not sure of the reason until Brown Fox had picked up the turkey by its neck and handed it to the woman who had come to take it to the cooking area of the village. There was still the de-feathering and cutting up of the bird, but that would be handled by the woman and the cooks that worked with her. Rising from her sleeping mat Little Star saw that White Bear had gotten up and was walking over to the curtain trying to grab Brown Fox's left leg. He was still a little sleepy, but said "We wash?" Little Star was surprised to hear him speak to Brown Fox with a sensible question, although he had probably heard Brown Fox tell him many times before as they headed for water in the morning, "We go to wash!" She was proud that White Bear was beginning to reason and communicate, and Brown Fox had been important in developing those traits. She realized she loved him even more than she thought she could during the mating ceremony.

The plaza area of the village was not set-up for trading the way it had been the last time Little Star and Gray Eagle had visited. At that time there were long, thin, cut woven branches set on three stumps of a felled tree. The way it was set-up this time was the three stumps were the same stumps used those three summers past, but the branches that were set over them were not woven, as the leaves had long been dried out and fallen off. Little Star was glad that she had woven blankets to spread over the dried out branches. They could not set anything heavy on the blankets, so they set the pottery on the ground at the end of the branches. The seeds were the most sought-after items the villagers wanted. No! Needed! Brown Fox and Little Star made sure that the seeds were available to the villagers who actually worked in the fields. Flint was the second-most sought-after item, as the area around Green Stone was not known to contain much good flint. The flint was used by families in starting their fires for meals and lighting the short cotton wick stuck into animal fat in bowls to illuminate their hut interiors. Woven baskets, blankets, and jewelry made from the pretty green stones found throughout the area were traded by the artisans of the village in exchange for some of the heavier clothing that had been accepted in trade from the people of Long River. The men who had been hunters needed new arrow and spear points, as they had let their old ones fall into disrepair. The new points had been made by the knappers of Besh ba Gowah. Brown Fox and Little Star deftly steered the trading so that everyone got value for the trades they made.

The trading really never got brisk during the whole morning, and at mid-day, the meal of turkey, leaves, berries, and water was served. One of the gatherers had gone over to the bend in the river and brought back some watercress, although they had not brought back enough to allow anyone to have more than a few leaves. It did serve to lighten the mood of the residents, and some came over to thank Brown Fox for the gifted turkey. After the meal was finished, Brown Fox and Little Star decided that it would not be worth continuing to trade, announcing their decision to leave the next morning. Leaving the meal area, they packed up the trading goods, the items they had received in trade, folded the blankets over the frame of the travois, loaded the trading goods, and prepared to haul everything back to the hut after harnessing the travois to the young female wolf. The trading goods were stacked inside the hut, and the travois poles placed upright against the backside of the hut. They would stay overnight and leave just before sunrise. One of the cooks brought a small package of traveling food to the hut. Shortly after that, shaman Gray Cougar and Brown Bear came to say their goodbyes and thank you. Brown Bear apologized that his grandfather Big Bear was unable to come over, but he was feeling quite weak, and asked that they pray to the "Great One" on his behalf. After Gray Cougar and Brown Bear had left, Little Star and Brown Fox asked White Bear to lie down on his sleeping mat while they made their plans for leaving the next morning.

A short time later, after they had gone to their sleeping mats, they saw a streak of lightning through the doorway curtain and a sharp clap of thunder followed. It began raining lightly, then becoming more of a steady rain. During the night the frequency of the lightning and thunder increased in intensity with one lightning bolt seeming to shake the very ground on which they were lying. The thunder was almost immediate, and there was a gurgling sound that seemed to erupt from beneath them. Brown Fox jumped to his feet, brushed aside the doorway curtain, looked out and shouted, "Lightning must have hit the hill, collapsing it and a spring has begun to flow! The village has been saved!"

Other doorways to huts opened and the people rushed out to watch in amazement as the spring kept getting wider and deeper, and the water in the river began to flow toward the opening to the canal. The rain was still coming down in torrents, but the people were dancing and singing praises to the "Great One." This was a night never to be forgotten by the residents of Green Stone, nor the visiting traveling traders, Brown Fox, Little Star, and even White Bear, who was being held tightly by Little Star. The joy was almost complete until Brown Bear rushed over to shaman Gray Cougar, saying, "Please come over to our hut right away. Grandfather is coughing and can't stop. He is very weak and I am very afraid for him." The shaman went directly to the chief's hut, walked in and knelt next to Big Bear's sleeping mat. Big Bear had stopped coughing, but his body was lifeless and beginning to turn cold. There was no sign of breathing. The chief had walked the path while his grandson, Brown Bear, had gone out to get the shaman. At this village's finest hour, it had lost its leader. Joy turned to sorrow as word passed through the crowd dancing in the village plaza. All of the people went back to their huts unsure of what would happen next.

Shaman Gray Cougar arranged for four men of the village to tend to the wrapping of the chief's body in blankets found in the hut, but that meant that his grandson, Brown Bear, would have to find another hut in which to live. His mother lived next to the chief's hut with her other young son, and she realized that it would be her duty to take Brown Bear into her hut for the time being. Her mate, Brown Bear's father, had been killed by a cougar four years past. From that time, chief Big Bear had taken Brown Bear into his hut and been teaching him the duties of becoming the chief of the village of Green Stone. Would the villagers accept him as being the next chief at his present age of ten summers? This was the first question that entered Gray Cougar's mind as he began to make plans for the funeral of Big

Bear. He had much thinking and praying to do before he could answer his own question.

Meanwhile, because of the rain during the night, Brown Fox decided that it would be too dangerous to leave Green Stone the next sunrise as there may be flooded washes, quicksand, and other dangers between them and the village of Besh ba Gowah. It was his intention to go back there to trade for more flint, as the need for flint had been so great at the village of Long River, and here in Green Stone, that they had very little flint remaining to trade. Because of the situation here in Green Stone, he and Little Star had traded almost all of the seeds they had brought with them, and now found themselves without corn, beans and squash seeds. The reeds, baskets, blankets and footwear they had received in trade in both villages would be valued by the people of Besh ba Gowah. And, that village had been having a good start to their growing season when Brown Fox and Little Star had left there almost three moons ago. Both Brown Fox and Little Star were curious to find out what had happened in the quest of Brave Beaver, Long Knife, Blue Nose and the six other men who were going to the village of Large House to rescue their families, and bring them to their new homes in Besh ba Gowah. Then too, Little Star had mentioned to Brown Fox that she had something very important to tell her sister, Little Fawn. She had not told Brown Fox what the secret was, but coyly said to him last evening before going to search for their dream catchers, "you will find out soon enough," then reaching over and kissing him on the nape of his neck.

It stopped raining just before sunrise. The clouds had moved toward the sunup direction, leaving the village under a grayish haze. The dust was settled by the rain, but the moisture above evaporated before hitting the ground, which left the woods and the bend of the river just an outline of what was physically there. It was a great feeling to wake up, go to the doorway, and see the river water once more flowing down the pathway that for years had delivered the life-giving water to the planted fields of corn, cotton, beans and squash. There was just a hint of green on some of the corn stalks already, and that meant that the crops would surely recover from the drought and produce the food necessary to keep this village alive. And, the spring right next to the village offered fresh, clean water for drinking. The "Great One" had listened to the pleas and prayers of the entire village including Gray Cougar, Brown Fox and Little Star, and the miracle renewed their faith in His healing.

A short while after their waking, someone brushed the curtain of the doorway. As Little Star went to see who it was, she saw that it was Brown Bear. He asked her if Brown Fox was in the hut, and when told he was, asked permission to enter. Little Star invited him in, and Brown Fox came over to meet him. They exchanged greetings, and sat down cross-legged on the sleeping mats. Brown Bear said, "I have the reward my grandfather promised you if your idea brought water to our fields and renewed the life of our crops. Although we did not have to dig for it, you were correct in suggesting that a spring below was the reason for the growing hill on the side of our village. I give you the bracelet that my grandfather promised you, and I thank you for the help you have brought to our people. Wear the bracelet proudly, knowing that my grandfather and the people of this village will always remember that it was your idea that explained the rerouting of the waterway. You will always be honored and welcomed here. Now I must leave, as shaman Gray Cougar asked to have words with me. The village council is gathered to ask me important questions, and I must not keep them waiting." Brown Fox was stunned by the gift, and in accepting it, said, "Brown Bear, it is a great honor to accept this beautiful bracelet worn by your grandfather. I will honor it always, and look forward to our next visit to the village of Green Stone." They rose from their sitting position and linked each other's forearms, as close friends often did when meeting or parting. Little Star held the curtain aside as Brown Bear left the hut.

Little Star walked over to Brown Fox and said, "You have made a great contribution to this village. Your name and reputation will live forever in the stories of this village, and I am very proud of you. It would not be right if we were to leave before the funeral of Big Bear, and before we find out who will become chief of Green Stone. It would be very unusual to have a young man such as Brown Bear become the chief, but he has been taught by his grandfather, knows the duties, and shows himself to be a man by his actions. The village would be very blessed to have him as chief for a very long time, and I am sure that shaman Gray Cougar will help him in every way he can." Brown Fox replied; "Yes, we should wait and attend the funeral for Big Bear. As for who will be chief, it could only be Brown Bear. He has courage, determination, and has learned the duties very well, I am sure. None of the other members have shown those traits that I have seen. I am sure the council will see fit to select him as the new chief."

After a short while there was a loud cheer that went through the village, just as the clouds drifted off to the sunrise direction, bathing the entire area in brilliant sunlight. Brown Fox went out to see what the loud cheering was about, walking toward the plaza area where the council had just announced the selection of Brown Bear as the new chief. Brown Bear was well thought of by the village, as was his father before him. After his father was killed by the cougar, the villagers felt sorry for him. But, as he grew, and was taught the duties of being a chief, they saw him grow from boy to a young man. He became familiar with each and every resident, their strengths and weaknesses, what they needed and wanted, and recognized the difference between the two. He helped out when help was needed or requested, and would listen to the council speaking during meetings, remembering the issues, and asking his grandfather in their hut for both sides of the issue. Discussing the issue with Big Bear was of particular importance, as his fresh input helped Big Bear decide his position, which was then taken to the next meeting. Even the young people of the village looked up to Brown Bear, although most were older than him. Yes, this was a good choice to just about everybody. The only person who did not think he was the person for the position was his own mother, Red Skies. However, she was not on the council. It was known by the residents that she was seeking revenge from the chief and the men who had accompanied her mate in chasing the cougar which had attacked their village. They followed it into the box canyon behind the village. As the three stalkers approached the side of the canyon, the cougar attacked, killing Brown Bear's father before the others killed the cougar with spears.

Preparations were being made by shaman Gray Cougar for two ceremonies, to install Brown Bear as the new chief and the funeral of Big Bear. In order to continue an unbroken line of chiefs, it was decided by the council that the new chief had to be installed before the funeral for the old chief. The hunters and gatherers suddenly realized they lived in a village that had a future and began searching for food, herbs and medicines. The residents who worked in the fields returned to their jobs, and the village returned to a normal routine that same day.

Brown Bear was installed as chief the second day after the council had met. It was Gray Cougar who conducted the ceremony. It began in the ceremonial pit, with Gray Cougar and Brown Bear standing face to face in the middle of the lower circle. With his arms upraised, the shaman called out to the spirits of the four directions to attend this most important ceremony. He took the ceremonial pipe in his hands, put tobacco into the bowl, and lit the pipe with a small lit twig that had been handed to him by the same man who had been holding the pipe. He began inhaling the smoke and exhaling in the sunup direction, then turned to each of the other primary directions doing the same, inviting the spirits of each of the directions to witness the ceremony. He handed the pipe back to the assistant, exchanging it for the eagle feather that was presented to him by the same assistant. He waved the eagle feather skyward, asking that the "Great One" and Father Sky witness the ceremony that he was conducting, then waved it from the ground skyward, asking that Mother Earth become a part of the ceremony as well. He handed the feather back to the assistant and placed his hands on the shoulders of Brown Bear. He announced, "Oh "Great One," Father Sky, Mother Earth, and all people and spirits in attendance, we have selected Brown Bear as the village of Green Stone's new chief, and he has accepted the position. Please help him to govern wisely, bless him with much wisdom and understanding, and help him guide us to our destiny." One of the village craftsmen brought an elaborately designed wooden bracelet to the circle and handed it to Brown Bear. He looked at it closely. It held a green stone the size of the tip of Brown Bear's little finger set into a hollowed out cup. The stone was held in place by four very small slivers of shaved gold-colored flat stones hammered into place to represent the four primary corners of the earth. The craftsman said, "The stone represents the village of Green Stone being the center of our earth." It was a fitting gift from the village to the new chief. In closing the ceremony, shaman Gray Cougar led Brown Bear to the chief's hut, adding, "May our new chief Brown Bear fill his hut with a mate and many children when he chooses." There were a few young girls that listened and thought of themselves as ready to help the new young chief in that regard. The village was now in the capable hands of the new young chief Brown Bear.

The arrangements for the funeral took much more time and preparations. The body of chief Big Bear had been taken to an abandoned hut near the back of the village. There were some trees behind the village, but not as far back as the box canyon in which chief Brown Bear's father had been killed. There were limbs on those trees that had good sturdy branches that would be used in erecting a pyre to hold the body as it was consumed by fire.

Four men were told to cut and trim four branches and lay them on the ground where the pyre was to be built with the top ends facing inward. Woven blankets would be tied between the inner ends of the four posts, and the wrapped body would be placed on the blankets. Holes were dug in the ground in which the posts would fit, suspending the body high above the ground. The next morning, the four men who had been helping Gray Cougar prepare for the funeral brought the body to the pyre, uncovered the body, and dressed it in a brightly colored vest and leather breechcloth. They took a long dry woven reed rope and placed one end inside the vest, allowing the other end to extend over the side of the pyre. At mid-day, the villagers assembled at the pyre to pay last respects to their old leader. Brown Fox and Little Star had brought White Bear, but were prepared to lead him away if he became noisy.

As Brown Bear arrived, accompanied by shaman Gray Cougar, the residents wondered, who will speak first, and what will he say? Shaman Gray Cougar started by saying, "This village has lost a great leader in Big Bear. We will miss his experience, but we have a new, younger chief now, with new ideas, a new purpose for our future. No one knew chief Big Bear better than his grandson, our new chief. Let him tell you of their relationship and how he will miss him more than any of us."

Brown Bear began, "My grandfather, Big Bear, did not expect that I would be the person to become chief after him. He had expected my father to become that person. However, my father died protecting all of us living in Green Stone, and grandfather took me into his hut and guided me toward being the chief he had seen my father to be. I will do my best to do the things grandfather expected my father to do, the things you need and want me to do, and the things I hope to do to make this village everything grandfather wanted it to be. I will need the help of all of you, and I hope that you will come to me when you see something that needs to be done that isn't being done. You will be guiding me just as my grandfather guided me. I pray that the "Great One" will allow my grandfather to help direct me to become everything he tried to prepare me to become." With that, he stepped aside and let the shaman take over. All those who were in attendance were impressed with the words and thoughts that had been expressed by Brown Bear.

One of the men assisting Gray Cougar came forward with the ceremonial pipe. It was lit and the shaman took deep puffs inhaling and exhaling toward the four primary directions inviting the spirits of those directions to join the ceremony. He then breathed smoke over the body to purify it before it would enter the happy hunting grounds. He exchanged the pipe for an eagle feather. He began waving the eagle feather over Big Bear, upward from the feet of Big Bear to his head in constant waves, encouraging the feather to take the spirit of Big Bear directly to the happy hunting grounds. As he finished waving the eagle feather, each of the four helpers took one of the posts, pulling them upright and placing the large, bottom ends into the holes dug for that purpose. The lit pipe was returned to the hands of Gray Cougar and he lit the end of the reed rope. The flames leapt high into the air, made the turn at the blanket and followed the rope between the chest and the vest of Big Bear. The return of dust to dust would be completed as the fire consumed the body, blanket and pyre. The ceremony was over, but as the group of villagers left, a lone eagle with the face of a young boy flew in a big circle above the pyre, unseen by anybody, swooped down and took the spirit of Big Bear skyward. The body and pyre were consumed by fire.

The evening meal was a small meal because the funeral ceremony took everyone away from their daily tasks, and there had not been enough time for the hunters and gatherers to have much success. There were two quail and one small rabbit that provided the meat, leaves from a bush that grew near the bank of the river beyond the bend of the river, and some watercress with a berry-flavored water drink. Brown Fox, Little Star and White Bear went back to the hut and began preparing for an early departure at sunrise the next morning. The trading goods were grouped so that they could be transferred easily to the travois, and the harness was laid out next to the doorway. One of the cooks brought over a small package of traveling food, thanking Brown Fox for everything that he and Little Star had done for the village, and saying his goodbyes.

The following daybreak found Brown Fox, Little Star and a walking young White Bear leaving the village of Green Stone. The male wolf was now the main animal doing the dragging of the travois. Since there was not much in the way of heavy cargo, it was planned that the male wolf would be in harness all that day. The female wolves were out hunting for food for the travelers and themselves. As they headed in the sundown direction, they were approaching hills to the hot winds direction, but the path they were using was quite level and clear of roots and vegetation. That meant that the female wolves were hunting beyond eyesight much of the time, and brought back smaller game. The travelers would reach Besh ba Gowah on the second day of travel from Green Stone, so when the young female wolf brought in a quail, that was enough to supply them the evening meal of meat. There were nuts and berries along the path the traveling traders were walking, so those were eaten as they were picked. The traveling food was eaten at midday, and the travel was stopped before the sun reached the top of the hill in front of them. It was over that hill and valley that they would approach Besh ba Gowah. White Bear had walked about a quarter of the way, and since the travois was not very heavy, Little Star had tied the chair seat to the top of the blanket on the travois. It was a welcome relief for her back, as White Bear was getting pretty heavy for her to be carrying.

As they settled on a level spot on which to camp for the night, the wolf was relieved of the harness and the travois was laid down as one side of the camp. There were some branches from a dead tree nearby that Brown Fox dragged over as the other side. There was room for the fire to be made in a small corner of the campsite that was protected from breezes, and the young wolves were stationed between the two sides of the camp, one at each end. White Bear had snapped some twigs from the smaller dead branches Brown Fox had brought over, so all they needed were the two dry pieces of flint to start the fire with. Little Star had been carrying two pieces in her amulet bag worn around her neck, but because they were in the leather pouch that hung between her breasts, and she had begun to sweat while walking, the flint became wet. They did have another set of flint in the trading goods, but it was not of the quality that she had been carrying. She went to the trading pack that the flint was packed in and began unwrapping it. In the meantime, Brown Fox had taken a small piece of wood, laid it on the ground and rotated a sharpened wooden stick into the wooden piece, having a very dried out, brown tree leaf next to the hole he was drilling. The leaf caught fire, and the flint wasn't needed. Little Star asked Brown Fox, "Where did you learn to do that? It certainly did work quickly." Brown Fox replied, "As a hunter, my father took me along on a few hunts, and I saw him do this on more than one occasion. Sometimes it takes a long time for the fire to catch. We were very fortunate this time." The evening meal was eaten, the sleeping mats spread with Little Star's in the middle. White Bear was very tired from all of the walking and fell asleep soon after lying down.

While Brown Fox and Little Star were lying down watching the moon and stars high above them, Brown Fox asked Little Star, "Of all of the stars in the sky above us, is there one that you would like to visit with me this night?" Little Star replied, "To pick out just one would be almost impossible. I would be happy to visit one with you. Do you see the end of the handle of the group that looks like a scoop?" Brown Fox agreed that he did see the one she was referring to, and said, "Let's visit that one and see if we can pour more love onto this world of ours." It did not take them long to scale the heights beyond the moon climbing toward the star at the end of the group now called the Big Dipper.

CHAPTER 7

As Brown Fox and Little Star were seen climbing the hill leading into the village of Besh ba Gowah the next day, one of the women gatherers saw them approaching and shouted out, "Ho ah, Little Star! It is so good to see you again. We have big news to share with you. Our village has grown since your last visit, and will be growing even more soon. We welcome you, Brown Fox and your son White Bear. Come, I will guide you into the village." As they drew closer, they recognized it was Pretty Sky, the woman whom they had first met in the fields at the village of Large House, then had found along the path-way between the Thunder God's mountain and the village of Besh ba Gowah, to which they had brought her. She had found her mate, Brave Beaver and her brother, Long Knife, living in Besh ba Gowah, as they had escaped the village of Large House four summers before.

Little Star called out, "Ho ah, Pretty Sky! We are so happy to see you again. Have you given up working in the fields and become a gatherer?" As they approached her, Pretty Sky came forward and hugged Little Star, saying "I value you as a sister, and want you to know I am with child. Working in the fields was getting harder for me, as the bending, hoeing, scraping and picking below my belly was hurting me. I just could not reach the low-growing beans and squash anymore. So, I decided to join the gatherers to bring in berries, leaves and nuts that grow in areas that I can reach more easily. I left my basket back there where I first spotted you coming up this trail. I will go back and get the basket, then accompany you into the village."

As they entered the village, the people who lived closest to the trail shouted their "Ho ah's" to Little Star, Brown Fox, and even White Bear who had hopped off the travois, grabbing the hand of Brown Fox and walking in next to him. It was over three moons since they had last been in this village, and they could see the village had new homes built and occupied. Little Star and Pretty Sky had been talking as they walked toward and into Besh ba Gowah, with Pretty Sky inviting the three traders for the evening meal at her new home. Pretty Sky had told Little Star that the quest to bring the women and children from the village of Large House had been successful. She had not had time enough to tell what method was used to lure the armed guards away from the entrance to the village, but Brave Beaver and Long Knife would tell the story to them that evening.

As word spread that traveling traders had entered the village, Gray Fawn and chief Koko-Who-Travels came walking from the center of the village toward them. Seeing that it was Little Star, Brown Fox and White Bear, they walked a little faster and met them near the ceremonial pit. Chief Koko-Who-Travels spoke first saying, "Ho ah, and welcome back, Brown Fox, Little Star and White Bear. We are surprised to see you return so soon, but happy that you have come back. We have much need for some of the trading goods that you offer. As you can see, our village is growing in number of villagers and new huts. The women and children who used to live in the village of Large House have joined us, and we must prepare for more children as the mates resume traveling to the moon and stars again. We will need baskets, blankets, bowls, clothing, footwear, and pottery. Have you received those items in trading with villages you have visited since leaving here?"

Brown Fox answered, "Ho ah, chief Koko-Who-Travels, we are happy to return to your village. We bring you the good wishes of your former shaman, Red Wolf and his mate Yellow Moon who live in the village of Long River. Their daughter, Full Moon is just as pretty as you had told us she was. It was good for Little Star to see her brother Red Wolf again, and we all enjoyed the chance to visit with my mother and father too. The trail was long and hard as we traveled to the village of Long River where they needed the good flint you had traded to us. In fact, they took almost all of what we had been carrying. They did trade baskets, blankets, clothing, footwear, and pelts for the flint. We have much of what you will need for your new members. After leaving there, we traveled to the village of Green Stone, which was suffering from a change in direction of the water for their growing crops. Also, chief Big Bear walked the path while we were there, but his grandson was selected to become the new chief, and rain helped to restore the flow of water to the fields. That village should regain its health and begin to grow again. We are happy to be back in Besh ba Gowah, and look forward to trading the items your villagers need."

While the men were talking, Little Star and Gray Fawn had been talking together too. Little Star told Gray Fawn, "Brown Fox and I have been mated by my brother, shaman Red Wolf in the village of Long River. You were right in suggesting that a stranger may not be what Brown Fox needed or wanted for his first flight to the moon and stars. We have been growing closer to each other, hearing and learning each other's needs and wants, and I have found him to be a wonderful partner on all of our flights. It is with great pleasure I announce to you that I am again with child, this time the seed of Brown Fox grows within me. The shaman Gray Cougar of the village of Green Stone told me that I would deliver a daughter." She did not want to tell Gray Fawn the rest of what Gray Cougar has said about the daughter living a difficult and short life. That was a pain she would have to bear by herself, and pray to the "Great One" that the prediction might be wrong.

Gray Fawn said, "I am very happy for you Little Star, my sister. Do you have an indication as to when the baby might come? You are much too small for it to come soon. How many moons did the shaman say you would have before delivering the baby?" Little Star replied, "He told me that it would be seven moons, but that is down to between six and seven moons now. I have not told Brown Fox yet, but I think he may have had a dream catcher telling him about it. He talks about, and takes on, more responsibilities as we travel. He spends much time with White Bear, teaching him many things a young boy should learn, and has become White Bear's best friend. I am so very proud of both of them."

The group had reached the visitors' hut, and Brown Fox had begun to slip the poles from the harness, and remove the harness from the wolf. As the travois lay on the ground, White Bear walked over to the wolf and began rubbing its side and patting its head. The new members of the village had not seen a young boy approach a wolf before, and were amazed at how calm everyone was when the boy began brushing the side and head of the wolf. Questions and comments were asked and made among these new residents such as, "Aren't his mother and father concerned that he might be attacked by the wolf?" "Is the boy not afraid of the wolf which is almost as big as him?" "The other two wolves are just watching for an opportunity to attack the boy." But as they watched, the other two wolves walked over next to White Bear, rubbing their sides against his bare legs and looking for attention from him. He continued to brush the fur on the head of the wolf that had been unharnessed, and with his other hand patted the others on their heads one at a time. These residents had a new respect for all three traveling traders, which now included the boy, White Bear.

Brown Fox began to unload the trading items from the travois and White Bear took his sleeping mat from the pile, carrying it inside the hut after brushing the curtain aside. As he did so, a squirrel came running out from inside the hut, and the young female wolf stepped on its tail as it tried to run by it. Caught as it was, the wolf bent down and picked it up between its sharp teeth. The squirrel was quite fat, and in trying to get loose, twisted its body so that its head slipped between the teeth of the wolf and it met its end. The lifeless body of the squirrel flopped to the ground. White Bear had returned from inside the hut, bent over, picked up the dead squirrel's body and handed it to Little Star. Had they been traveling between villages, this would have been skinned, the meat cut out, and they would have had squirrel for dinner. Inside a village, other meats would be offered and served. Here in the hills around Besh ba Gowah, deer, big horned sheep, quail, rabbits and turkeys were usually the meats of choice. As a result, Little Star handed the squirrel to Pretty Sky who had walked alongside Little Star and Gray Fawn as they went through the village. After thanking Little Star, she went off to the hut in which she and Brave Beaver lived, began skinning the squirrel, cutting off the meat, and putting it into a pottery bowl. Then, she added water to keep the meat cool. It would be prepared for eating on another day when there would be no guests. After living without much food to eat at the village of Large House, she was not about to waste anything. She began preparing a meal of quail, beans, squash, mushrooms, and berry water for her traveling trader guests, Brave Beaver and herself.

Since it was well past midday when Brown Fox, Little Star and White Bear had arrived at the village, it was too late to prepare a big feast for them. Although Gray Fawn invited them to evening meal at chief Koko-Who-Travels' and her hut, Little Star felt obligated to tell her that they had been invited to Pretty Sky and Brave Beaver's hut after meeting on the trail. The group in front of the hut left to return to their huts and prepare for their evening meals. Brown Fox, Little Star and White Bear finished unloading the travois, stacking the items inside the hut, feeding the birds some berries, while the wolves enjoyed the leftovers of the quail from the evening before. Then the traders walked over to Brave Beaver and Pretty Sky's hut.

Brave Beaver and Pretty Sky's hut was beside the hut in which Little Star's brother, shaman Red Wolf and his mate Yellow Moon had lived. It was now the hut lived in by Bright Sun, the new shaman-in-training, and his teacher, Blue Stone. As Brown Fox, Little Star and White Bear approached the area, they heard chanting coming from Bright Sun's hut. The chanting was the beautiful sound of a young boy, asking the "Great One" to bless the village with a good harvest in the next moon cycle. The chant spoke of the beautiful sunshine, warm weather, and shimmering water to flow through the furrows of beans, corn, cotton, and squash. They waited outside Pretty Sky's hut listening as Bright Sun asked for success in finding bushes filled with berries, trees with many nuts, and mushrooms growing in the meadows around the village. Lastly, he had seen in his dream catcher great big, shaggy animals on the faraway plains in the sunrise direction, and he implored the "Great One" to bring them to their village to help feed the people of their village, if meat became scarce. The sound trailed away as he began to hum in soft tones toward silence. Little Star turned to Brown Fox and said softly, "Surely, this is a holy man in a young boy's body! He shall be an important shaman for many, many summers."

Brown Fox brushed his hand across the doorway curtain at Brave Beaver's hut. Pretty Sky held the curtain to the side, greeting each of them as Brown Fox, Little Star and White Bear entered. Brave Beaver had just finished pouring the berry water into the pottery cups. The food had been prepared and set on wooden plates which were placed in a circle on top of a stiff woven reed tray set on three short blocks of wood at knee high level. There was room for everybody to sit cross-legged around the tray. Before eating, Pretty Sky said a prayer, "Oh "Great One," thank you for sending these three traveling traders to the place at which they saved my life, thank you for allowing them to bring me to this village where I found my mate, Brave Beaver, and thank you for allowing his seed to fill me with a child. We pray to you to help us become all we can be, and be invited to join you and all of our family and friends in the happy hunting grounds when you call us."

The food was eaten, and the talk turned to the stories each family had to tell. Brave Beaver told about the rescue of the women and children from the village of Large House. It happened just as Bright Sun had foretold at the evening meal during the traveling traders' last visit. Brave Beaver began saying, "Storm clouds filled the skies to the hot winds direction. They seemed to whirl upwards, picking up dirt, dust, brush and stones high into the air, moving over large areas coming toward us. The curtain of dirt, dust, brush and stones was so dark we could not see through to clear skies behind the storm. We had taken woven scarves of cotton to put over our faces, just below our eyes. We shielded our eyes by putting our hands over them with a slit between fingers as the only way we could see. As the storm moved into and over the village of Large House, we saw the two guards who had been standing at the gate be picked up and thrown deep out into the desert. That gave us time to run through the gate, go to the homes of our families, and guide them out of the village. There was no sign of Black Coyote or the other two guards. We kept moving until darkness overtook us, but by then the storm had wiped out our tracks. From that time on, we came straight through the desert, and up over the dripping springs mountains to Besh ba Gowah." Brave Beaver went on, "We are so happy that we could bring our families to this village where we were accepted, and we plan to earn our right to be here by helping Besh ba Gowah grow into a large village. Having not been together for such a long time, the other men and their mates have planted seeds and we will increase the village by six more babies soon."

Brown Fox was curious and asked, "Brave Beaver, has anyone gone back to see if the village of Large House is still standing? In such a storm, walls and homes could have been torn apart. It is interesting that the two armed guards were lifted up and carried away by the whirling winds. The others may have been inside their living structure, but that could have been destroyed as well as other parts of the village." Brave Beaver answered, "We were just happy to leave that place, and never looked back to see if the village was still there. It brought back so many bad memories, and we were trying to get as far away as we could before anyone knew we had been there. Nobody wanted to look back. It was a long journey, and we are glad to be away from that place, and chief Black Coyote. May he starve to death in that prison he calls a village. All of us have started new lives here in Besh ba Gowah, and are happy to contribute to the growth and values of this village." Pretty Sky spoke up saying, "I am so proud of our men who went to rescue the women and children who still lived there. The "Great One" has blessed us and given us a second chance at living worthwhile lives."

Little Star was the last to speak up and said, "With what you have gone through, it is only correct that you live in a village that believes and works toward peace and harmony." Changing the subject, Little Star continued, "After you birth the baby, will you return to the growing fields, or will you remain a gatherer?" With no hesitation, Pretty Sky said, "I will return to the growing fields. It is my passion to plant seeds in the ground, watch the water flow through the furrows, nurturing those seeds into food that feeds, or helps clothe the village. I see the work of the "Great One" as the crops grow and are harvested. That is where I want to be."

It was time for White Bear to go back to the hut and get ready to search for his dream catcher. Brown Fox and Little Star thanked Brave Beaver and Pretty Sky for the evening meal and the conversation they all had enjoyed. After walking through the doorway, Little Star grabbed one hand of White Bear and Brown Fox grabbed the other. Together they began walking toward their hut, lifting White Bear off of the ground and swinging him back and forth as they walked. As they reached the hut the sun was just setting behind the big trees near the waterfall.

The next morning, the sky was just beginning to show the lighter shades in the sunrise direction as Brown Fox, Little Star and White Bear left the hut to go wash in the brook. Their gray messenger birds in their hut had wakened them, and they were thankful that they were the first ones to arrive at the brook. The water was cool, but it would not remain that way for long as the sun would warm the water later in the day. As they walked into the water together, White Bear looked at his reflection as he bent over. He giggled and said "Me." Brown Fox and Little Star laughed and Little Star said, "Yes, you!" It was a wonderful feeling for Little Star to see her young son growing into boyhood. She wondered how White Bear would feel about having a sister. She still hadn't told Brown Fox about her being pregnant, but it would become evident to him very soon. He had been wondering about her not telling him it was time for her flow as they continued to visit the moon and stars together regularly. It would only be a few more days and she would begin to show, certainly before the next moon.

Returning to the hut, Brown Fox asked, "What are your plans for the next few days? I know that we will be trading here for a day or two, but when were you planning on leaving, and where will we go from here?" It was a question that Little Star had asked herself, but did not have an answer. She had hoped that Brown Fox would have a plan and that he would tell her either today or tonight. She answered, "I have not really given it much thought as there is much of the summer ahead of us yet. We have not gone toward the cold wind direction to see our old friends from the village of Canyon of Walnut Trees. It would be pleasurable to see Black Bear again, and find out if his father, Black Raven still walks Mother Earth. Black Bear made the beautiful jewelry that when the quartz stone was cut in a certain way it shone in the brilliant colors of the early sunrise sky. It would be a long, hard walk, but I think the trading might be well worth the effort."

Brown Fox replied, "I think that you just want to go see Black Bear and trade for some of his sparkling jewelry and forget about me. Is that your plan?" The last part was said in jest, and they both chuckled over the thought. Little Star said, "I would not know what to do without you, and White Bear would be lost without his playful father. The "Great One" knew what he was doing when he had you follow Gray Eagle and me after we left your village of Long River. You have been so important to me, to Gray Eagle, our family. I must tell you that you will become a father of another child soon. I have been told by shaman Gray Cougar of Green Stone that I am with child, and it is by your seed. The baby is to be a daughter, and should be born in about six moons."

Brown Fox was stunned, and did not know what to say. He had no idea that his seed would be acceptable to Little Star and that the "Great One" would bless them with a child so soon after they were mated. Right now, he knew that he would have to load the travois with the trading goods, harness up one of the wolves and lead the wolf and trading goods to the village plaza where the displays would have to be set up. As these jobs were being accomplished, Brown Fox's mind was in a whirl. 'What did a father have to do while the baby was born? Where would they be when the baby came out? Would they be in a village or out in the desert or mountains?' All of these questions raced through his mind, and he knew that he would have to ask someone who knew the answers, but whom? Normally, a shaman would be the person who could answer questions pertaining to the blessings people received in the form of birthing children. Bright Sun was young and would not have knowledge of such things. Ah, but chief Koko-Who-Travels' mate, the present shaman of Besh ba Gowah, Gray Fawn, would know. After all, she was present when Little Star birthed White Bear and Flying Eagle. She had knowledge and experience. She would be able to advise him as to what had to be done. He would have to find a time to see her when Little Star was not around, ask her what was expected of him, and how he could help.

The setting up of the displays was done before Little Star arrived. Brown Fox had become very good at arranging the goods in a way that presented the items with the lowest value on the ends of the display. Little Star was expecting that the baskets, bowls, cups, pottery, wooden forks and spoons would be good trades, as the new families that had moved in from the village of Large House would need those items. The center of the display was where the most valuable trading goods were shown. The woven mats, clothing, a flute that had been received in trade in Long River, footwear and pelts were the most prized items displayed; but partially hidden in the middle next to the leather dresses and vests were the beautiful green stone jewelry and polished stones received in trade from the craftspeople of Green Stone. Brown Fox and Little Star had ideas of what these items would bring in trade. The items in the middle would bring in the finest flints to be found. The bells made by the Besh ba Gowah craftspeople would be valuable at other villages they would be traveling to, as well. They would also try to trade for seeds as the village of Green Stone had taken all of what they brought along from the village of Long River. Little Star and White Bear arrived as Brown Bear was finishing the arranging of the pottery.

The first group that came to the table surprised both Brown Fox and Little Star, as they were the hunters. There was a hunt leaving shortly after sunrise and the hunters did not want to miss out on trading. Besides, they knew having first choice of the offerings would allow them to make the first trades and help to set the values on trades that would follow. The footwear was the first area the hunters moved toward, and it was not long before the first three trades were completed. These hunters had trailed and killed a bear and traded the bearskin for three pairs of goat skin slippers with young rabbit skin sewn expertly to the insides of the slippers. They would be more comfortable and outlast by many moons the slippers they were now wearing. One of the hunters looked closely at the flute, mentioning to the man standing next to him, "Maybe we could make it sound like a deer looking for a mate, a turkey, or a javelina, and get some of that meat that is always trying to avoid us." He picked it up and blew into it. The sound was shrill and not at all like any animal sound, and the men around him, and even Little Star, laughed. He put it down and moved along the line toward the spear points. There he found two that he traded some flints for, making Brown Fox and Little Star happy. That was the first flint offered so far, but they wanted, or needed, much more. There were a few other trades between the hunters, Brown Fox and Little Star, but none were for more of the flint that was known to be available from this village. They would have to wait for the artists and craftspeople to get to the display. They were the ones who would be looking for the colored stones, the pelts, clothing and maybe the flute, and be willing to trade some of the flint they had collected. There were also the gatherers who would find some flint sticking out of the ground, and bring it back with the berries, fruits and herbs they had found, and would bring that to trade.

Bright Sun came strolling up to the tables accompanied by Blue Stone, his teacher. He had heard the shrill sound of the flute, and came to look at it for himself. He picked it up and began to cover the holes with his fingers before putting it to his lips and blowing into it softly. The flute seemed to wail in a peculiar way, and his breaths made the sounds soar and then come back down in a pleasing cadence. It reminded Little Star of the way that Kokopelli had made the flute fly like bird songs on a slight breeze, and these sounds took her back to her early life in Besh ba Lakado. Blue Stone was surprised to see and hear her student play an instrument with such clarity, picking up the sounds of chirping birds, the lilt of a melody, and finally, a sound like the rushing water of the waterfall. As he withdrew the flute from his lips, he looked at it from the mouth piece to the tip, rolling it between his fingers, lovingly caressing the sides as a man might caress the body of a woman. Bright Sun turned to Blue Stone and said, "This flute I must have for myself. It allows me to sing like a song bird, soar and screech like an eagle, fall like a pleasing rain and become a part of Mother Earth that sings the praises of the "Great One." Please trade for it, teacher Blue Stone." Blue Stone turned toward Little Star ready to ask what goods would be needed to trade for the flute, but Little Star said, "Blue Stone and Bright Sun, I could not accept anything in trade for the flute. It came alive in your hands and from your lips. I have not heard anything as beautiful since my spirit father, Kokopelli, played his flute. This flute belongs to you. I give it to you, as only you can master this instrument of flight, song, and waterfall."

An appreciative smile passed through Bright Sun's face, and his eyes spoke of thanks and understanding while looking deeply into Little Star's eyes. For a second in time, she was completely within his power. She had never felt this way before, but was completely at peace within herself. As he glanced away, she regained her feelings, and turning, said to Blue Stone, "Bright Sun is destined to become a great shaman. He has many talents at a young age. You are preparing him well to serve all mankind. Thank you for bringing him here to the trading display. Is there anything you might need from our trading tables?" Blue Stone answered, "No, there is nothing I need at this time. Bright Sun has been my whole life since I first met him two summers past. It has been a wonderful experience to be able to help him prepare to become the shaman of Besh ba Gowah. He has special powers to be able to see into someone's very soul, giving them a comfortable, peaceful and good feeling, encouraging them to live within the "Great One's" rules, and to become more aware of the people and things around them. I have felt this power surround and enter me for all this time. I need no more than what has been given me through Bright Sun. Thank you for asking." With that,

Blue Stone and Bright Sun walked back through the village to their hut.

The trading day went by quite quickly as the artists, craftspeople, gatherers, and the other residents, young and old, came to see what items they needed to trade for, as there was no assurance that other traders would be coming their way before the harsh winter would envelope them in this high desert location. There were many items that were brought over by all of the members of the village, but the ones that were most active in trading were the women who had been rescued from the village of Large House. Their mates had new huts built, but the furnishings were sparse, and the baskets, blankets, pottery, wooden forks and spoons were all items that were needed to make the huts more livable. There was much flint brought as trade goods by the villagers, as the hills around them were full of the valuable material. The knappers had been busy preparing sharp arrowheads and spear points, and some brought in raw pieces of obsidian, the material from which the sharpened points were made. These raw pieces were highly sought after by the people far to the sundown direction, where the great sand dunes were located according to Kokopelli. Yes, Brown Fox and Little Star enjoyed a very successful trading day at Besh ba Gowah.

All during that day, White Bear and the three wolves had been playing with the young boys from the village. They had been playing near the brook, with the boys petting the wolves, chasing them around in a circle, and letting the wolves nip at their heels as they turned to allow the wolves to chase them. Two of the older boys and one young girl watched over the group playing in the sun. When they got hungry at midday, the girl ran over to the brook where there were some berry bushes growing and picked enough to give each of the children a few to tide them over to evening meal. The wolves caught a small prairie dog coming out of its hole and the three wolves had a light lunch of their own. White Bear enjoyed being with other young children, and had gotten used to sharing their toys with them. He was learning to communicate with them and that night he began to speak in more complete sentences. He was developing a personality through his contacts with boys of his own age, and a few that were older. He still looked at Brown Fox and Little Star as guiding him in most things, but when he was playing with other boys, and the wolves, he was treated as an equal. It was a feeling that he had not had before, although he had played with other children; but these boys were playing without adult supervision. The boys and the girl watching them allowed them to be themselves, separating them only if a small disagreement occurred. The wolves watched over their playmates as well, but the other boys were aware that to the wolves, White Bear was part of their family.

As the evening meal ended, Brown Fox took White Bear to the hut in which all of the trading goods were stacked and the sleeping mats had been laid down, while Little Star went to visit with her sister, Gray Fawn. White Bear began to tell Brown Fox of the fun and games which he had been playing with the other boys and the wolves. Brown Fox listened proudly as White Bear told of the games of tag, the boys chasing the wolves, and the wolves chasing the boys, during the day of play. The enthusiasm he showed in telling the story was exciting to Brown Fox, who recalled his younger days and how much he enjoyed playing with his friends. He began to think of what White Bear was missing by being the son of traveling traders, who arrived in villages one day, stayed for two or three days, and then moved on to the next village. Were he and Little Star being fair to this young boy? Would he ever truly have friends that he could remember in his later years? Were they giving him a chance to be a boy? Was he happy moving from village to village, not knowing a home, or home village? He would speak with Little Star about this after she returned from visiting with Gray Fawn in chief Koko-Who-Travels' and her hut. Then, it was time for White Bear to seek his dream catcher.

As Brown Fox sat cross-legged on his sleeping mat, he began to think about how he enjoyed being back in the village of Long River with his parents, family and friends, and how his feelings regarding Yellow Moon came flowing back. He had many dreams about her when he was young. He had dreamed that she would wait for him to grow up and mate with him. He had no idea as to what mating was all about back then, but he knew that he had wanted her near him forever. When Yellow Moon left the village in search of her promised mate, Brown Fox felt a huge loss. She had left the village, and him, and he would never hear from her again, never see her again. And then, Gray Eagle and Little Star arrived as traveling traders and told the village that they had seen her. Yellow Moon was the mate of the shaman at a village called Besh ba Gowah, many days in the sundown direction. Oh, how Brown Fox had wanted to go find her and have her become a part of his life again. The two traders had brought a wolf to their village, and that fact had presented an opportunity to him. The wolf seemed to enjoy his company, and although he was afraid of the wolf at first, Brown Fox began to feel that the wolf was a way to get back to see Yellow Moon. He had asked his father and mother for permission to become a traveling trader, a profession much desired by young people, as it offered travel, excitement and opportunity to see many different things in this huge world. Permission had been granted and Brown Fox followed the traveling traders and the wolf out of the village of Long River toward wherever they were going next. That night he caught up with the traders, and climbed over the barrier that surrounded their camp. The wolf had detected his intrusion and "wuffed" softly, alerting both Gray Eagle and Little Star of his presence. From that night onward, Brown Fox had become a part of the traveling trader business, from which he learned a lot about people, their needs, their wants, and the differences between them. Now, he had to balance the needs and the wants of a young boy, a boy who thought of him as his father, a mate, whom he loved dearly and had been the daughter of the great traveling trader, Kokopelli, and his own needs and wants. But, what was it he needed or wanted?

Brown Fox was deep in thought as Little Star entered the hut, sitting down cross-legged on her sleeping mat across from him. She reached for his hands with hers, looked deeply into his eyes and said, "Brown Fox, I must tell you something of great importance. Gray Fawn has told me that we must be in a village at the time the baby arrives. That means in about six moons we must be in a village that has a woman who will help bring our baby out. Gray Cougar told me that we would have a daughter. I know that he was right to tell me I was with child as my flow did not come as it should. That is why we have been able to visit the moon and stars so many times after leaving Long River. Gray Fawn, the shaman here, told me that it will not be easy birthing this baby. I leave the planning up to you as to when and where we should plan to be as we near the time of birthing the child."

Brown Fox was overcome by the news. He thought to himself, 'Why now, when I am worrying about the life we are leading our son into? Is this a sign from the "Great One" to find a village in which to become members? Should we give up our dreams of traveling to the great waters in the sundown direction, the ice far to the cold wind direction, the jungles in the hot wind direction, and the unending sands in the sunup direction? What is it that we should do? If we do settle into a village, where should we go? We are known in Besh ba Lakado, Besh ba Gowah, Green Stone, and Long River. Which of these would be best, and what would I do to become a part of the village? Could I become a hunter, gatherer, artist, craftsman, or work in the crop fields? I am so confused.'

Little Star was feeling confused too. She did not know what Brown Fox would think or say, and she was worried. It was quite a lot to place on him; a son who knew him as a father image although he was not the father, a mate who was with child, his child, and an indefinite day in the future that would bring forth his own child, a daughter, according to shaman Gray Cougar of Green Stone. She thought to herself, 'What will he say? What can he say? Is he happy to become a father? It will take time after the baby is born to resume our traveling. Will he want to resume traveling or will he want to settle down in a village? What will he do if we do go to live in a village, and what will I do? What village would he want to live in, Long River, Besh ba Lakado, Green Stone, or Besh ba Gowah? Or, will he leave us and resume the traveling trader route by himself? I must wait for his answer.'

The dream catchers of Brown Fox and Little Star that night were mixtures of the good dreams that were remembered the following morning and those bad dreams that passed through to be forgotten in the light of day. Waking up, Brown Fox looked straight into the eyes of Little Star, who had been waiting for him to waken. Her soft brown eyes were filled with concern, as his eyes focused on hers. He reached over and put his hands softly behind her head and stretched over toward her, kissing her on the lips softly. He said to her, "You are beautiful to wake up to. I hope that you had good dream catchers, as I dreamed of holding our daughter in my hands for the first time. She was so little, so delicate, so pretty just like you. I pray that we find a good woman at a village to help you birth the baby. I will be there with you, doing everything I can to help. We must rest for a day or two here, and make plans to be where you want to be when the baby is ready to come out. Is that agreeable to you?" Little Star answered, "That is agreeable to me, but are you sure you want to return to being a traveling trader. With a new baby we would not be able to travel as fast, nor quietly. Maybe we should find a village to become a part of, at least until the baby becomes old enough to travel. During the time in a village, you and I would need to work for the good of the village, and White Bear would have an opportunity to grow friendships and learn what it is like to live in a home." She continued, "There is also the possibility you may want to go on without me, White Bear, and the baby, when it comes. The children and I would have to live in a village that would accept us, and we would have to wait for your return, if you so chose. We need to think about these choices and discuss them before we go too far from the areas which we know."

Brown Fox had listened to everything Little Star had said, following each thought she expressed, until she got to the last part about him traveling on alone. At that point he became confused. He realized that he wanted to be a successful traveling trader, but he loved Little Star very much. And, he was happy being a father to White Bear, teaching and training him to be a responsible young boy. With a new baby, it would be true that they could not travel as far, as fast, or quietly. But if he were to leave them in a village while he traveled on, he would consider himself to be selfish. Little Star had wanted to be a world traveler, and had been the reason that Gray Eagle had left Besh ba Lakado. It was she who had come from the seed of the great Kokopelli, the most well-known traveling trader of their world. Questions tumbled through his mind with no answers, just more questions.

Brown Fox was speechless for a few moments before he answered, "I understand your concerns, and I will confess, mine are similar to yours. I had not given any thought to leaving you in a village while I continue on a traveling trader route. We are partners in life as well as in business. We both have dreams of seeing the great waters and to walk the sand dunes in the sundown direction. We have not seen the plains where the huge, shaggy animals are said to live. I have never wanted to travel to see the large ice mountains in the cold wind direction, but I would like to travel down to where the huge stone buildings stand in the hot wind direction. To see these things alone would never satisfy me. You are my mate, and I want to share everything I see or enjoy with you. We will seek a village in which we can stay while the baby is born, and allow it some time to grow before resuming our quest to see these wondrous things. Those are my thoughts."

White Bear had wakened and rolled over closer to Little Star. He had listened to the last part of what Brown Fox had been saying, but had not interrupted. He understood the part of finding a village in which to live, and he thought of the friends he had made here in this village over the past few days. He tapped Little Star's arm and asked, "Me go to play now?" A smile crossed Brown Fox's face, and he looked at Little Star to see if her answer would be the same as his, if he were to answer White Bear's request. Little Star saw the smile and replied, "White Bear, you may go out and find your friends to play. You may want to take the wolves with you." In a flash, White Bear had gotten up, brushed the curtain to the side and darted out through the doorway. Brown Fox came over closer to Little Star, taking her in his arms and they traveled to the moon and stars together, although it had become bright daylight outside. A late and satisfying arrival at the moon and several stars was shared.

The second day of trading was much slower than the first. Brown Fox and Little Star had taken more time eating their morning meal, not rushing over to the plaza to set-up the trading goods displays. The hunters had not yet returned from the hunt of the previous day. Some of the gatherers had accompanied the hunters, while the others had been sorting the berries, fruits, herbs, leaves, mushrooms, and nuts they had been accumulating. The people who worked in the crop fields had checked the water in the furrows, and done some weeding the day that the traders had entered the village. It was a day of rest for most of the village. It seemed like a quiet peace had entered the village relaxing everyone who was there.

A woman's voice began to sing a well-known song of praise to the "Great One," and as she began the words to a second verse, the beautiful sound of a well-played flute floated through the village. Several other voices joined in, singing the words, adding to the melody. Even the birds in the air stopped chirping as if listening to the enchanting song of prayer. As the sounds filled the village, a huge eagle swooped down from high above. But the eagle had the face of a boy, and as it flew low over the village, it seemed to gather the sounds of the song of praise into its great wings, and flew back up, up, up, until it disappeared out of sight. Those of the villagers who had seen the eagle had much to talk about, among them a very, very happy Little Star. She had seen her Flying Eagle again! As she gazed across the village, she saw Bright Sun still playing the flute with Gray Fawn, Eagle Wing in her arms, next to him singing, their eyes searching for the retreating eagle boy.

Brown Fox had been behind the trading tables when he had heard the flute playing and the singing, and looked up as the eagle's shadow passed over the front of the tables. He saw the huge wings and the boy's face quite clearly, and recognized an older Flying Eagle than he had known. Although he had heard the stories of the eagle boy told by a number of people, this was the first time he actually saw the face. When they were trying to find the way down the hill before entering the village of Long River he had seen the body of the eagle, but did not see the face of eagle boy. This time there was no mistake, it was definitely Flying Eagle.

White Bear had been playing with his young friends and the wolves while this was happening. The two older boys and the young girl were watching the children closely as they were playing near the brook. The eagle screech from above alerted all of them to turn and watch the eagle diving down toward the village and rising majestically back into the sky, climbing higher and higher before disappearing. White Bear raised his hands into the air as if he knew it was his twin brother, the eagle boy who had come to visit. None of his playmates, nor the young boys and girl, knew the story, nor was close enough to actually see the face of eagle boy, but they remembered, and retold, the story many times over the next many days and summers.

The trading day came to an end shortly after midday, as Little Star joined most of the villagers gathered around the hut of Bright Sun and Blue Stone. The villagers who remembered Little Star telling her story of the eagle picking up her infant son, Flying Eagle, from the meadow grasses above Besh ba Lakado, asked her whether it had been Flying Eagle who had visited them. She said that it was definitely Flying Eagle, and that she, and the village had been blessed by his visit.

At the evening meal that night, extra prayers were said by Gray Fawn, the shaman. She was elated to have seen eagle boy, and thanked the "Great One" for sending an indication of His pleasure in hearing the song of praise to Him. Her prayer was, "Thank You "Great One" for sending down Your eagle boy to carry up to You the music and song we played and sang in Your praise. We thank You for the food You and Mother Earth have provided for the health of our bodies, and we pray for Your help in guiding us to the happy hunting grounds You have readied for us."

Chief Koko-Who-Travels rose to thank Bright Sun and his own mate, Gray Fawn, for playing and singing so beautifully. He also thanked those villagers who had joined in the song of praise. He mentioned "It is a great honor to have the mother of eagle boy with us in this village. We feel blessed to have her and her family with us, and want to tell them that they are always considered to be members of our village of Besh ba Gowah. As you may remember, Little Star gave birth to twins here but three summers ago. Her first born son, White Bear is here with her, while the second son you had the privilege of seeing today as eagle boy. It was a great sacrifice for her to lose Flying Eagle, eagle boy, at a very young age, but he was taken from her for a very important reason. He has become a messenger between the "Great One" and us, His people." Bowing toward Little Star, Brown Fox and White Bear, he continued, "Please accept out thanks for your great sacrifice." Sitting down cross-legged in front of the large round wooden platform, the young girls responsible for bringing the food out for the meal began by bringing out the chief's meal first, and then the rest of the inner circle was served.

White Bear had jumped up after finishing eating, and ran back to play with the wolves tethered next to the hut. A few of the other young boys saw him rubbing their sides and the fur on their heads, and they jumped up to join him. They could be seen from the ceremonial pit enjoying their time with White Bear and the wolves.

Little Star began talking with Gray Fawn and Blue Stone about the growth of the village and the hunting party and when they were expected to return. Brown Fox, chief Koko-Who-Travels, and Bright Sun began talking about the village and what services might be needed that were not being met. Brown Fox was searching for something that might be of help to this village, as he had come up with an answer for Green Stone's problem with redirecting water to where it was needed. He could see a need for more permanent homes made of stone rather than the huts in which the villagers lived. While in the village of Large House, he saw that the big house of Black Coyote's was built from the clay that was beneath the topsoil on the valley floor. That clay, when combined with water, could form air and water-tight binding of the walls and roof between the stones used to construct the walls. With thick branches stretched across the top of walls, then covered with the wet clay pitched to run down the sides, there would be no leakage into the interior. Also, that type of building would last a very long time.

Brown Fox mentioned the idea to chief Koko-Who-Travels, who appeared very interested in trying the concept, and asked Brown Fox, "Can you build a building in which we can store supplies for the winter?" Brown Fox answered, "I can put up a large building for that purpose, but it might take me several days to accumulate the materials." Bright Sun suggested that two men be assigned to help Brown Fox, and that was agreed to by the chief. Since the trading between the traveling traders and the villagers had been completed, Brown Fox volunteered, "I will start collecting materials for the project after sunrise tomorrow." Chief Koko-Who-Travels asked Brown Fox, "Whom would you like to have work with you?" Brown Fox answered, "Brave Beaver and Long Knife, Pretty Sky's mate and brother, have had experience working on this type of building at the village of Large House." They had gone with the hunting party the previous day, but were due back the next day. He expected that question to be asked, and thought that Brave Beaver and Long Knife would be of great help in working with the caliche mud he hoped to locate beneath the soil in this upper desert. They would have some knowledge of the mixing and texture of the mud to be used in erecting the buildings.

He began to plan what the building of a new Besh ba Gowah village might look like. 'All doorways would need to open to the sunrise direction, for the morning light and inviting the warm rays of sunshine from sunup to midday. The roof and walls would reject some of the heat and the hot rays of sunshine after midday during the summers. The cold winds normally would blow from the sundown direction during the cold winters, and the walls and roofs would help to keep the interior warm. The tallest building could be a two story building that would house the lookout's room with spirit windows in the four primary directions.'

His designing mind was racing as he began to see the village being built all around him. 'This is an important job. I would be doing something that will last for a very long time. People will look upon the buildings and say "This village was built by a great person; one who knew and respected Mother Earth, understood Father Sky, and offered much praise and honor to the "Great One." This woman's father, Brown Fox, was the builder." This woman's father, Brown Fox?' He was projecting his unborn daughter into his future! His thoughts turned to the realization that he was turning a large supply building into a whole new village, a new career, and perhaps a new home for himself and his family. 'What has happened to my dreams of becoming a far-ranging traveling trader? What will Little Star think? What am I thinking?'

Little Star, Gray Fawn, and Blue Stone finished eating, and their conversations. Standing, they began to urge the men in their lives to get up and return with them to their huts. The men all rose with Chief Koko-Who-Travels joining Gray Fawn, Brown Fox took Little Star's hand, and Bright Sun bowed to Blue Stone and they all began walking toward their respective huts. As they walked, Brown Fox was thinking how he could raise with Little Star the subject of the task he had offered to perform for the village. He began, "Little Star, I have been thinking about what would be best for you and our baby, and have come up with an idea that we stay here at Besh ba Gowah until after the baby is born. I have offered to build a supply building for the village. This supply building would be built in the same way as the big house at the village of Large House. Chief Koko-Who-Travels has offered me the help of Brave Beaver and Long Knife, both of whom have had experience in building large buildings like the one that will be needed here. It would benefit you too, as you would not have to walk the many days between villages, up and down mountains, across the hot deserts, and through valleys, facing dangers all the while. Also, you would have Gray Fawn here to help you in birthing our daughter. I would feel more comfortable knowing that you will have help during that great event. This will also allow White Bear to grow up with friends. It is important for young children to have a place they can call home, is it not? We can always resume the traveling trader route later, after the baby is born."

Little Star was stunned to hear of the plan that Brown Fox had told her. There were some ideas he mentioned that appealed to her, but she was worried that they would never resume the trading route. She had a lot of faith in Gray Fawn, both in delivering the child and being the shaman for the village. The idea of White Bear growing up with other boys of his age was very important. The help that Brown Fox could be to the village was a great gift to the people of Besh ba Gowah. Also, she was becoming aware of the gifts that the "Great One" had given her mate, the ability to engineer improvements and new methods of doing things to make living easier for themselves and those around them. She answered him saying, "Brown Fox, I am very proud of you, and the many things you have done for us and others. You have great abilities to help villages with problems and in making the villages a better place in which to live. I agree with you that Besh ba Gowah is a wonderful place to have White Bear develop friendships and that Gray Fawn will help me in birthing our daughter. Your offer to build a supply building will only be the beginning. When the villagers see the advantages of the sturdy walls and roofs, they will want their huts to be of the same materials and quality. But, do you really believe that we will return to the trading route and see the great waters? If you are sure that we will, I will gladly become a member of this village until that time."

Brown Fox was happy to hear of Little Star's decision to remain in Besh ba Gowah until they could resume their traveling trader route. He would begin his scouting for materials to build the supply building the next morning. He was hopeful that the clay underneath the ground here would be similar to that in the desert around the village of Large House.

Shortly after sun-up, after he, Little Star and White Bear returned from washing at the brook and having an early morning meal of bird eggs they had found in a nest next to the brook, Brown Fox began looking for the clay beneath the grasses found beside the path leading to the waterfall. He did not find any clay under the grassy area. Next, he tried in a rocky area near the top of a small hill above the village in the hot wind direction. There were trees up there, but not much moisture in the ground, so that was a possible location for the clay. Once more, he was proven wrong. A third and fourth location were checked, but no clay like that found beneath the desert. He was not discouraged as he remembered the boulders and stones used in the cave dwellings at Besh ba Lakado and Long River. They were the type that could be cut and shaped to fit tightly together. Using sand and water as packing, the shaped stones could be stacked to form straight walls, with sap from cactus and pine trees filling any remaining gaps. There were many suitable boulders and stones nearby that could be used to form the supply building, and many homes as well. By the end of the day, Brown Fox had changed his ideas on how to change the village from round mound-style huts to square straight-walled buildings that would last a very long time. Roofs would be pitched from front to back or back to front allowing rain run-off to be channeled and flow down a path behind the village into the crop fields. Snow and ice melt would do the same, giving the crop fields extra moisture for spring planting.

While Brown Fox was doing his searching and discovering new ways to do things, Little Star was learning some of the methods that were being used by gatherers. The vegetation in the upper desert was different from the area around Besh ba Lakado, and she had never been too active in gathering back there. She had gone with Pretty Sky, who taught her how to get the best mushrooms, berries that were edible, nuts that had different uses, and how to find and pick the sweetest leaves from the bushes and trees in the area. She had always let Gray Eagle or Brown Fox do the hunting and gathering, but she had a new respect now for what they had done for her.

White Bear and his young friends had a very pleasant day, running through the village, alongside the brook and playing tag with the wolves. He certainly was enjoying himself, and tired himself out just after midday.

Brave Beaver and Long Knife arrived back in the village just before evening meal.

They each brought back a good-sized turkey, with Brave Beaver bringing back two quail and Long Knife a large rabbit. They each did the de-feathering, Long Knife separating the rabbit pelt from the meat and Brave Beaver preparing the quail for the pottery crock while their mates prepared their evening meal. They were told by their mates that Brown Fox wanted to see them, so they ate first then walked over to the hut in which he, Little Star and White Bear were just sitting down to rest. Everyone had had a pretty busy day, so there would not be a long conversation this night. Brown Fox told Brave Beaver and Long Knife that the three of them were going to build a building in which to store supplies, and how he expected it to be built. After asking them if they had any suggestions, they decided to go ahead with the ideas of Brown Fox, and begin accumulating the materials the following day. The supplies were to be fitted onto the travois and dragged to the site of the building. They built that building in one moon, and began to erect homes using the same methods. Brown Fox ordered two more travois to be built for the wolves so that supplies could be brought to the sites faster.

Day after day, the village moved ahead with the building of homes by Brown Fox, Brave Beaver, Long Knife, the wolves, and the families for whom they were being built. Much searching for and collecting the necessary materials preceded working together toward assembling the homes.

The hunters were out looking to bring as much meat in as they could. The gatherers were bringing in everything they could as well, including the reeds and lily pads from the brook, berries, leaves, mushrooms, and collecting the last of the watercress. It was never enough as no one could guess how harsh the winter would be, and they wanted the village to be prepared. The crop fields were being harvested as well, and most of the cotton had been picked and stored first. The beans, corn, squash, and tobacco which grew wild near the edges of the fields were brought into the new building and it was nowhere close to being filled.

Everyone was told to continue to bring in whatever they found, as the needs of the village were greater with the number of new residents being added. A herd of deer came close to the village one day, chased by a cougar, and the hunters were able to bring down three large bucks, two does, and a fawn struck by an errant arrow. The largest pottery containers were used to preserve the venison in water, hoping that it would remain good for several moons into the winter. Brown Fox and the three wolves went out one day, just to get away from the work of building. They brought back three large rabbits and a big-horned sheep. White Bear had learned enough to help skin the rabbits, but Brown Fox skinned the sheep.

Time was counting down to the date of Little Star's delivery of the baby. Winter had come and gone, and she, Brown Fox and White Bear were quite comfortable living and working in the village of Besh ba Gowah. She worried as her dream catchers gave no indication of the name she should give to the child. Prior to the twins being born, her mother White Moon came to her dream catcher and told her what names to give the sons, but she had not been visited for that purpose yet. She was suffering great pain when bending over, and her back felt as if a knife was stabbing her constantly. Even lying down at night was uncomfortable, and she rolled from side to side trying to find relief.

Nothing seemed to work, and she finally went to see Gray Fawn at her new home. She brushed her hand across the doorway curtain and Gray Fawn asked her to enter. She saw that Bright Sun was there, and as she entered he looked directly into her eyes. She felt the same feeling as she had those many moons ago, feeling completely within his control. As he spoke, the sound came to her as if in a dream. He said, "Little Star, you are in need of a special medicine. Please go to the supply building and request one single mushroom, oil from the inside of an aloe leaf, and bark oil from a pine tree. Bring it back to me here, and I will apply it to your back. It will soothe your pain. Do it now!" He looked away, breaking the spell he held over her. Unsteadily, she left the building and walked tentatively to the supply building. Requesting and receiving the items Bright Sun had commanded her to bring, she walked back to Gray Fawn's home. She was admitted by Gray Fawn, and she handed the items to Bright Sun. He told her to remove her clothes and lie face down on a sleeping mat that had been prepared for her. She did as she was commanded, and he went to his knees next to her. Applying the ingredients to his hands and rubbing them together, he began chanting and rubbing her back with his hands. At first the concoction seemed to burn into her skin, but gradually it seemed that the pain was flowing from her body into his hands. His hands became so soft and gentle that she almost nodded off to a peaceful sleep, one that had eluded her for several nights. As he pulled his hands away from her body, she felt very relaxed, and just wanted to lie there and go to sleep, but she knew that she must go back to the hut in which she, Brown Fox and White Bear lived. She knew that she had to do that as she had been smitten by the care Bright Sun had shown her and the power she knew he had over her. She put her elbows under her and raised herself up on her elbows and knees. She felt Bright Sun look at her, no, through her, right to her soul. She reached for her clothes, hurriedly put them on over her head, pulling the covering over her milk-filled breasts and big stomach. He could not possibly think of her as being pretty, but she knew that she wanted him to. She thanked him for the medicine and the massage, and told him how much better she felt. Blushing, she excused herself and left Bright Sun and Gray Fawn, exiting the home. On the way back to her hut, she felt that her body had betrayed her, but she knew that it was more than that. Her mind wanted him to continue to touch her, to caress her, and to take her to the moon and stars with him. She felt ashamed as she knew that he was less than half her age, but he had such power over her.

She arrived back at the hut, and saw that Brown Fox and White Bear were inside trying to cover a small toy figure of a bear. A piece of wood had been whittled down to a bear standing on four legs, and they were trying to cover it with white rabbit fur. The figure was not longer than Brown Fox's hand from wrist to the tip of his middle finger. The small piece of white rabbit fur was more than enough to cover the entire toy. It would be wrapped over the back, cut and would be stitched on the underside. The wooden legs would be left uncovered. It would be a nice toy for White Bear to own and play with. It was a complete surprise to Little Star that the two of them had gotten that far without her knowing they were working on something together. It made her very proud that Brown Fox was taking such an interest in White Bear, and trying to help him become more involved with boys the same age. She bent down to see the figure and praised their handiwork, saying, "Brown Fox and White Bear, that is a fine toy bear that you are making together. I would hope that you were careful in using the knife to shape the body. I don't see where either of you are bleeding, so you must have been careful. When you fit the rabbit fur over the bear, may I stitch it together for you, or do you want to finish the project by yourselves?" Brown Fox looked up at Little Star and replied, "I think that the three of us working together can get the job done. White Bear, should we let your mother help us finish the toy?" White Bear answered, "Yes papa, let her help." The toy was finished the following day, and White Bear was happy to show the boys his new toy bear. The toy got passed around, and was never completely white again.

The work that was being accomplished by Brown Fox, Brave Beaver and Long Knife was getting much attention. Both men and women of the village began to help in building more of the new stone homes. They were able to complete a home from start to finish in twenty days, with the men selecting the materials, the wolves transporting them to the proper sites, women bringing in the sap from the cactus and pine trees, and even the older boys bringing in sand and water to be used before covering the jointed areas with the sap overlay. The cold winter became more comfortable for the occupants of the new homes.

Then, one night Little Star received the dream catcher she had been waiting for. White Moon, her mother appeared to her, and said, "Little Star, Mother Earth beckons to the spirit inside your body. Mother Earth is saying "Come be a part of me. I will feed you, clothe you, help you grow, and give you purpose. By way of Father Sky, the sun, moon, and stars have united with me to provide you form, life and breath. Join with all of us in praise and honor to the "Great One," our Creator, and He will grant you peace and harmony during your walk of life." Little Star asked her mother White Moon, "Mother, what should I name my baby?" White Moon replied, "Call her Far Star, as she will have a very hard and short walk of life. I must leave you now, but Kokopelli and I are very proud of the way you, Brown Fox, and White Bear have been living your lives. Be aware of changes that may occur." And then she was gone!

Little Star woke with a start. She had so many questions she wanted to ask her mother White Moon. Why would Far Star have a hard but short life? What should she watch for in trying to keep Far Star safe? Is there any chance that Far Star could live a comfortable and long life if she, Little Star, would watch her closely? What danger would put Far Star in trouble? What changes would occur? The questions kept bothering Little Star the rest of the night, and she did not sleep any more after that.

Four nights later, during the middle of the night, Little Star woke Brown Fox and said, "Brown Fox, it is time. Please go to Gray Fawn and tell her that the water has broken. She will come over for the blessings before birth and ask you to get items together for the birth of our daughter. Please hurry now. White Bear can stay here sleeping until Gray Fawn wakes him up and sends him to find you."

Brown Fox hurried over to the home of chief Koko-Who-Travels and Gray Fawn, brushing the curtain of the doorway to their home. Gray Fawn had been expecting Brown Fox to be coming to get her, as she had seen signs of Little Star's belly begin to drop lower, indicating birth to be close. Brown Fox told her that the water had broken and asked her to hurry over to their hut, then went to prepare the items that Gray Fawn had mentioned to him in their previous meeting. Gray Fawn gathered up the already prepared pipe, feathers and a small bag before exiting her home and walking toward Little Star's hut.

Upon arriving at and entering the hut, Gray Fawn saw that White Bear was still sleeping next to his mother, Little Star. She gently woke him and asked that he go out and look for Brown Fox who would be sitting beside the fire next to the ceremonial pit. White Bear got up and walked outside while Gray Fawn began preparations for praying the birthing prayer and blessing the mother and child before the delivery. She reached into the small bag, withdrawing four small stones and began by saying, "Little Star, become as one with Mother Earth and grandmother moon, as both have birthed children. Mother Earth has brought forth birds, animals, plants, trees, and water, while grandmother moon has brought clouds, snow, wind, ice and rain into being. Place two of these stones into each of your hands and squeeze them hard as the baby comes out. There is a black obsidian stone that allows a believer to see through the pain to the light and joy on the other side, a green stone that reminds us of Mother Earth's goodness, green grasses and trees, quartz to remind us of the purity of the air that surrounds us all, and the red ocher for the blood of your new child. These stones will help you bear the pain of delivering your new child. Honor the "Great One" after this child is born by placing these stones in your medicine bag to be worn around your neck to remind you of the great gift you have been given." Then she took the long stemmed pipe she had brought with her, lit the tobacco contents of the pipe bowl, inhaling and exhaling several times before breathing the smoke upward toward the "Great One," to the four primary directions, then toward mother earth, inviting all of them to be present at the birth of a new life. Finally, she inhaled and exhaled the smoke over the reclining body of Little Star, onto the extended stomach, and the area from which the baby would be delivered. Laying the pipe down on the floor next to her, she picked up the eagle feather. She waved it twice from the top of Little Star's head downward toward the stomach and beyond to the place of delivery. This was to encourage the baby to leave the mother's womb and enter the world, where the deities would see it for the first time and introduce its spirit to the "Great One."

Little Star's contractions started as the feather was laid down next to the pipe. Gray Fawn went to the doorway and summoned Brown Fox to bring the hot water he had been warming in the cook's fire pit near the ceremonial pit. The water was brought to the doorway, handed to Gray Fawn, and Brown Fox led White Bear to the side of the brook to wait for word of the birth of his daughter.

The birthing was extremely hard on Little Star. Since she had birthed the twins over four summers before, her body had changed, and birthing became more of a challenge to older, weaker bones and tissue. Although she wanted this baby desperately for Brown Fox and herself, she realized it would be their baby for only a short while, according to the words of shaman Gray Cougar and her dream catcher of her mother, White Moon, four nights before. She didn't know the reason the daughter would not be theirs to cherish for a long time, but she believed both the shaman and her mother, as he was a holy man and she was a spirit. Neither could lie. With a huge effort, the baby was loosed from Little Star's loins. Gray Fawn held the baby in one hand, cut the cord, placing a small leaf on the belly where the cord had been cut. Getting a small cough from the tiny body was not hard to do. Gray Fawn then washed its body and laid it on the small blanket on the floor next to Little Star's right leg. It was a small baby girl that fit into a corner of the blanket. She was so small that Gray Fawn worried that she would not be able to suckle from Little Star's breast, and may starve to death. She showed the baby to Little Star, holding it in one hand as she tipped Little Star's head to the side. Little Star smiled, but she could see the baby was much too small, and she, too, worried about trying to feed the baby. Gray Fawn reached over and squeezed a drop of milk from Little Star's right breast and put the drop on the tip of her little finger. Opening the mouth of the baby, she rubbed the drop against the upper lip allowing it to be absorbed into the baby's mouth. She did that twice more, and the baby had its first sustenance.

Gray Fawn asked, "Little Star, what will you and Brown Fox call your daughter?"

Little Star answered weakly, "Her name is to be Far Star. We will love her and care for her as long as she is allowed to be ours, but she will travel the path sooner than her normal walk of life, according to my dream catcher. Please don't tell anyone I told this to you. I have not even told Brown Fox." Then, it was time to bring Brown Fox in to see his daughter. Gray Fawn went outside and loosened the tether on the older female wolf, telling her to go and bring Brown Fox and White Bear back to the hut. The wolf took off at a trot, going down to the brook, and the man and boy raced back with the wolf arriving just ahead of Brown Fox. He did not wait to brush the curtain, but walked in, dropped to his knees looking down at the tiny baby lying next to Little Star. Seeing how small she was, he wondered if she was real or a small toy. She was breathing, so she was alive. This was Little Star's and his daughter. He looked up at Little Star who had a forced smile on her face, and he knew not all was right. White Bear had entered the hut and sat on his haunches across from Brown Fox. He saw the baby, and asked "Who is that?" Little Star answered, "This is your little sister, Far Star. She is a very tiny baby, and we must take care of her. Will you help us with that?" White Bear said, "I will help." He lay down on his sleeping mat and went back to sleep.

Little Star needed sleep. Far Star needed rest. Brown Fox was worried about the forced smile he had seen on Little Star's face, and even more concerned about what he had seen in her eyes. Her eyes had always been alive, always bright anticipating life. Her eyes looked tired, not willing to accept what life had just offered. Brown Fox bent over to kiss Little Star and told her how much he loved her and their new daughter. He said, "Close your eyes and get some sleep. You need to rest and get your strength back. I will see you later today. I must get ready to go to work now." Leaving the hut, he walked back to the brook taking his worries with him as he walked into the water to bathe and pray.

Gray Fawn went over to a corner of the hut where the trading goods were stacked, and sat down cross-legged. She must stay and watch the baby and Little Star, and pray for both. She was the shaman of Besh ba Gowah, and it was her duty to pray with and for its inhabitants, and she knew that the people in this hut needed her prayers to the "Great One."

As her prayers, honor and praise were offered, a thought came to mind that left her stunned. 'I have seen the effects that Bright Sun has produced on the face, in the eyes, and to the body of Little Star.' Gray Fawn had been shaken by the communication between their eye contact while sitting in her home those days before. 'It was as if he had taken over Little Star's mind and body, making her unsteady on her feet, and unsure of normal movements. Was his will commanding her spirit to perform or understand certain expectations? He was being trained to become the shaman by Blue Stone, a most respected teacher, but what were the signs of his authority over this woman who is a sister to me? Perhaps it was a healing influence, an assurance of peace and harmony to return to her life. After all, she had been suffering pain when she came looking for relief, and she had left after telling him how much better she felt. Yes, that had to be it.'

CHAPTER 8

The next morning the village was told of the arrival of its newest member, Far Star, daughter of Brown Fox and Little Star, and sister to White Bear. The village rejoiced as another resident meant additional protection, another gatherer, cook's helper, or crop harvester. This village was growing in numbers and living methods. The way things were being done now was far different than just the summer before. What made the big difference? It was the arrival of Brown Fox, his new ideas, and the wolves. They had brought the village together, working, playing and living in peace and harmony. The homes that had been built would offer warmth during the winters, the new supply building would be able to hold enough food, clothing, water, ice, and everything they would need for the whole winter. That same supply building would offer a cool interior to keep the food cool during the hot summers, and store many items that were used year around. However, the village was getting large at the expense of the diminishing meat sources, the crops in the fields were limited by the irrigation canals, and the hunters and gatherers would be forced to travel farther from the village to find the items the village needed. This was not a concern to anyone in the village that day. They were happy for the new life born to their village.

Gray Fawn had not gotten a lot of sleep the night before after watching Far Star and Little Star while they slept. Her worries about the power that Bright Sun exerted over Little Star were forgotten as daylight appeared through the curtain of the doorway. As Little Star awoke she complained of pain in her back and sides. Gray Fawn asked, "Would you like me to massage your back and sides to ease whatever pain you have before you try nursing your new daughter?" Little Star answered, "It might help if you wouldn't mind. I don't have any of the ointment that Bright Sun used when he rubbed my back and sides the other day. He had asked me to get one mushroom, oil from the inside of an aloe leaf, and bark oil from a pine tree from the supply building. I will remain lying here while you get the items he used." Just as Gray Fawn rose to leave and get the items from the supply building there was a brush at the curtain of the doorway. From where she was sitting, Gray Fawn saw that it was Bright Sun who was requesting admittance. She said to Little Star, "It is Bright Sun who is asking permission to enter. Do you want me to allow him to come in?" Little Star looked confused, but replied, "Yes please allow him to enter. He must want to see Far Star, the newest member of the village."

Gray Fawn went to the curtain and holding it to the side, invited Bright Sun to enter. As he entered, Gray Fawn saw that he had brought a small pottery jar of what looked like the ingredients he had used to massage the back and sides of Little Star the day they had all been in Gray Fawn's home. Looking down at Little Star, he said, "I have brought the medicines which I used to relieve the pain in your back and sides the other day. Have the pains returned, and if they have, would you like me to give you a massage to remove them?" As she turned to look up at him their eyes met, and she felt the power envelope her once more. She was under his influence, unable to break the eye contact. She answered, "Yes, Bright Sun, I would appreciate anything you can do to make me feel better." Another brush of the curtain and Gray Fawn looked out to see chief Koko-Who-Travels standing outside. She went to the curtain, holding it to the side, and the chief said, "Gray Fawn, there has been an accident at one of the homes that is being built. We need you to come there right away. Hurry please, as one of the men is badly hurt." Gray Fawn wavered for just a moment before she rushed out of the doorway and followed her mate, the chief, toward the scene of the accident.

Little Star's heartbeat soared. She would be alone with Bright Sun, and only her newborn daughter would be with them. Bright Sun was still looking deeply into her eyes, not allowing her to turn away. He asked her, "Are you able to turn over on your stomach and allow me to massage your back and sides?" She answered, "Yes, I should be able to do that." She twisted her body to the left away from her sleeping daughter, and toward the kneeling Bright Sun. This broke the eye contact, but she still felt his eyes penetrating the side of her head. He was kneeling with his knees at her hip level and was able to gently fold the back of her top up past her shoulders, rolling it behind her neck. She had her head turned toward the door, the side on which he was kneeling, but she was not seeing anything in front of her. Her mind still held the intensity of his eyes looking into hers, seeing into her very being. She did not understand what was happening, but she knew that he was studying to be a shaman and would not be able to do anything wrong. He reached his hand into the jar, bringing out the mixed ingredients and began applying it to her back. The first sensation was the burning feeling going into her skin, but slowly, expertly, his hands became softer, working the mixture into the painful places in her back and sides, making them feel young and alive again. She felt so relaxed as his hands softly caressed her back and sides that she was ready to go back to sleep. Then, there was a brush of the curtain at the doorway. Bright Sun looked up and saw that it was Gray Fawn who had returned, asking permission to enter. He rose from his knees and held the curtain to the side, inviting her to enter. From the look on her face, he could see she had bad news. Gray Fawn suggested that Bright Sun might be needed at the scene of the accident. He said his goodbyes to both

Little Star and Gray Fawn before wiping his hands clean and dry on a woven cotton cloth, and leaving the hut.

Little Star turned over on her back, feeling much relieved of the pain she had been feeling before the massage. She saw the look on Gray Fawn's face and wondered what it meant. Gray Fawn began to tell what had happened at the building of one of the new homes where the accident occurred. She said, "Little Star, there has been a terrible accident at one of the new homes that Brown Fox was helping to build. One of the large stones that was being placed into the wall fell out and crushed the leg of a worker. That worker was Brown Fox. We have lifted the stone off of his leg, but the leg is damaged badly, and it doesn't appear he will ever be able to walk on it again. We are bringing him back to this hut, and I and Bright Sun will minister to him, trying to heal him as best we can, but don't expect us to completely heal him."

Little Star heard what Gray Fawn had said, but she found it hard to believe. Brown Fox had always been the rock she relied on, the one person who brought back the dreams she and Gray Eagle had together, her mate whom she had just made a father, and a man whom she loved deeply. Her disbelief turned into sobs and then bitter crying. How could this happen just as she had made him a proud father? He had become so successful, an important member of this village, and now this?

At the site of the accident, men who had been working on building the new home were lifting Brown Fox onto the travois, and Brave Beaver was going to lead the wolf over to the hut in which Little Star was lying.

Gray Fawn was speaking, and Little Star was wiping her eyes trying to bring her feelings under control. Gray Fawn said, "Little Star, it would be better for Brown Fox if he did not see you grieving. We all know that it will be hard for you and Brown Fox to remain in good spirits while the two of you are healing, but this village will do everything it can to help you. The most important thing you can do is raise White Bear and Far Star to become good people. Your beliefs, dreams, love and understanding of people will help them see the good in others, and they can become important parts of our village of Besh ba Gowah."

Just then, the wolf pulling the travois had drawn up to the doorway of the hut. Brave Beaver and Long Knife carefully lifted Brown Fox out of the travois, and Gray Fawn held the curtain open while they carried him into the hut and laid him on his sleeping mat. He had been given some medicine that made him unconscious, but a cry of pain escaped his lips as they straightened out his crushed left leg. Seeing her mate be brought in and laid down on his sleeping mat beside her was heartbreaking for Little Star. She thought to herself, 'We were so happy and proud earlier this morning when he came in to see our newborn daughter, and now he is lying unconscious next to me. I cannot understand how this could happen to Brown Fox and me. We have been so happy from the time we left Besh ba Lakado, coming here before going to the village of Long River and seeing Red Wolf, Yellow Moon, and their daughter, Full Moon. Meeting Brown Fox's family and being mated there, coming back through Green Stone where Brown Fox discovered the reason for the change in the flow of the river water, and coming here to build new homes for these villagers have all been important times during our lives.'

As these thoughts were going through Little Star's mind, White Bear came running through the curtained doorway, pushing it inward and to the side as he entered. His big smile was the brightest thing that could have happened at that moment. Little Star looked up at her handsome young son who was getting close to four summers now. Just seeing his smiling face helped her swallow the tears she was beginning to feel entering her throat as she would not want Brown Fox to see them on her face if he awoke from his unconscious state. White Bear said, "Hi momma, why is papa home sleeping? He has a bad hurt on his leg, doesn't he? When it gets better we can go out to play, can't we?" Little Star kept her feelings well hidden, and replied, "Yes,

White Bear, the two of you will be able to go out and play when his leg gets better. Where were you and with whom did you play today?" White Bear answered, "Some of my friends went over to the waterfall and looked down at the river below. It is a long way down there, and the water moves very fast and loud." Little Star had a bad feeling about that waterfall as she remembered Night Star, the twin sister of chief Koko-Who-Travels, had fallen, or jumped, to her death from the top of that waterfall. It was said that she now lived on a tall pinnacle of rock far to the cold wind direction, watching for naughty children that she kidnapped and took to live with her, never to be seen again. She told White Bear, "Do not go back to those falls anymore. They are dangerous and I don't want you to fall and hurt yourself. Promise me, won't you?" Without a real thought of obeying, he said, "I promise."

The evening meal was brought to their hut by two of the serving girls. Brown Fox woke from his forced sleep and looked down at his crushed leg. It hurt him terribly, but he tried to keep the pain within him, not allowing Little Star to hear his inward crying. He had been so sure of that huge stone fitting in the wall, and the helper he had lifting the stone into the hole slipped as they were placing it over the opening when it came tumbling back at him, landing on his left leg. The leg had broken in several places, and the main bone had been crushed. He had heard one man say, "There is no hope of him walking again," as they lifted the stone from his leg. He thought, 'Why did it have to happen? Why wasn't I more careful? Why did it happen just when I am becoming an important part of this village? What can I do to regain my health, strength, and be able to go back to being a traveling trader again?' Little Star's and his dreams had been shattered in an instant.

Later that evening, a brushing of the curtain brought a surprise visitor to the hut. Little Star asked White Bear to admit the person who had brushed the curtain, and in walked Bright Sun. Little Star was embarrassed, as she thought that he had come to visit her. That was not the case. He said as he came in, "I am here to see Brown Fox. I have a strong medicine that I have made to help heal his terrible wounds. It may not make the leg like new, but I am hoping that it will allow him to walk again." With that, he walked over and knelt next to the crushed left leg. Putting his hand into the solution that was in the pottery dish he had brought with him, he applied some of an evil-smelling jell to Brown Fox's hip, and down to his ankle, around the entire leg. The leg had lost all feeling, so Brown Fox felt no pain when the jell was applied. Then, Bright Sun wrapped the leg in a bandage made from lily pads found down by the riverside below the waterfall. Understanding that this young man, Bright Sun, had taken the path down alongside the dangerous waterfall all the way down to the riverside, and back up again, was a huge surprise to both Brown Fox and Little Star. Brown Fox thought, 'Why would he take that chance to go down there by himself just for me? He doesn't owe me anything. But if it works, I will be very grateful to him for what he is doing for me.' For the next few days, Bright Sun came twice a day, applying jell and wrapping the leg. There still was no feeling, but color was slowly returning to the leg indicating there was life and blood flowing where it had looked completely dead the day after the accident happened.

Upon Bright Sun's arrival each time he would attempt to make eye contact with Little Star, but when he arrived the second day she knew that she could look away as he arrived, and would look to the side when he left. Watching his every move while he applied the jell, she became familiar with the procedure, and told Bright Sun that she would be happy to take over the task when she felt stronger if he would bring the ointment to the hut.

As Little Star recovered from having the baby, she began applying the evil smelling jell to Brown Fox's leg on the fourth day, and kept up the twice a day medications. For almost a moon there were no indications other than the leg color becoming more natural-looking. Bright Sun and Gray Fawn visited often, checking on Brown Fox's leg, Little Star's return to health, and Far Star for her growth. White Bear became a helper to all of them, and Little Star was thankful for that. He would take the wolves out for a walk, allowing them to run for awhile before calling them back. It seemed he had taught them his language, or he had learned theirs. People of the village marveled at how he worked hard at helping around the hut and with the animals. Even his exercising the birds now and then was a common sight around the village. Another strange thing was that Bright Sun began to accompany White Bear on some of his duties. While they were together, White Bear learned a lot from Bright Sun and Bright Sun seemed to learn things from White Bear. Bright Sun was particularly interested in the way that White Bear controlled the birds and wolves. But Bright Sun taught White Bear about some of the medicines he made from the bark, berries, leaves, nuts, and plants that grew around the village.

At the beginning of the second moon, Bright Sun brought a stick that was forked at the top, and was long enough that when Bright Sun helped Brown Fox to stand, the fork at the top of the stick fit under his arm pit. Leaning on that stick, Brown Fox was able to stand and maintain his balance. A few days later, he began to take short tentative steps with Little Star beside him, walking just a few steps before he sat down just outside the hut. It was a start, and it buoyed his spirits tremendously. Over the next few days, Brown Fox extended his walking to a few more steps each day. It was extremely hard for him to get up from the ground grabbing the stick and pulling himself up until the fork fit under his arm pit, but it was progress. No one in the village expected him to walk again, but it had been Bright Sun who had the faith, courage, and determination to find a way to help Brown Fox return to becoming a useful member of Besh ba Gowah. The building of the new style homes continued while he lay in the hut, but now that he was out and beginning to see the effects of his engineering, he was much happier.

The men and women of the village were happy for Brown Fox, Little Star and White Bear, but still were concerned that Far Star was not growing as quickly as was expected. The efforts of Bright Sun were celebrated as the residents became aware of the help he had given Brown Fox. "He has become an accomplished shaman at a very young age." "His knowledge and experience are well beyond his age." "What he has done for Brown Fox and his family is remarkable." There was only one thing that bothered Little Star and that was that Bright Sun was paying less attention to her than to Brown Fox and White Bear. While the confidence and abilities of Brown Fox were being heightened, White Bear had spent additional time with Bright Sun, and she was left to care for Far Star. It was evident that she was not interested in becoming a caregiver, stay-at-home, mother. Blue Stone had come over with Bright Sun and Gray Fawn to check the progress of Far Star, and upon seeing the child being so small and helpless, Blue Stone offered to help Little Star care for Far Star when and if she was needed. It was a wonderful offer that came at the right time for Little Star.

The end of summer was approaching, and the need for additional gatherers was evident. The gatherers were extending the areas in which they were searching for the foods, medicine and other items that would be required by the village during the winter. Little Star would be a great help in finding items that would be farther away from the village as she had had much experience walking long distances and transporting heavy loads. And, she had the use of one of the wolves which could be harnessed to a travois, making the return to the village easier and quicker. Of course, she would use the older female wolf, the wolf that she had befriended along the trail from Besh ba Gowah to the village of Green Stone. She had not been out alone for many summers, but this was an opportunity for her to meet and face her feelings, taking on the questions and problems one at a time. She had to think about many things and decide what was best for Brown Fox, White Bear, her and Far Star. As she left the village for the first time, she had strapped the harness, the travois poles and the light-weight woven netting to the back of the adult female wolf so that it would not have to drag the poles and travois behind.

Little Star and the wolf walked toward the sundown direction and the dark canyon with the walls that reached over the pathway. She hated that area, but knew that just beyond there were the large cacti with their arms raised toward the "Great One." The thin staves that made up the skeleton of the tall cactus were often used to support the roofs during winter snows. They were light, but strong, long enough to stretch from front to back of the new homes. Many of the staves could be set into the travois and transported back to the village. They could be stored either inside or outside the supply building for use when they would be needed. There was little strength required to break them away from the dead cacti, but she would have to be careful to watch for spiders and other creatures that might try to hitch a ride in the travois.

She was thinking about those things as she was getting close to the entrance to the dark canyon when a "wuff" from the female wolf caused her to stop and look into the mouth of the canyon. She could see nothing, but heard some voices echoing through the opening. She did not want to face anyone inside the canyon, so she looked for a place to hide and waited for the people to appear. Finding a few small bushes to the side and above the entrance, she waited until two men came striding out of the opening, and she recognized them as being two of the armed guards who had protected the entrance to the village of Large House. It appeared as though they were following a pathway that was heavily used as they were constantly looking down at the ground following and pointing toward footprints. Little Star and the wolf were shrinking back into the shadows of the bushes, but the movement alerted one of the men to look in their direction. He saw a shadow behind the bushes, and gestured to his companion to stop. Little Star reached for the knife she was carrying and cut the straps holding the harness, travois and travois poles to the wolf's back. The poles fell to the ground making a clattering noise as they fell. She held the wolf around the neck until she saw the men advancing toward the bushes she was hiding behind. She allowed the wolf to leave her and confront the approaching men. The men stopped walking but readied their spears to throw at the animal. The distance between the men and the wolf was more than thirty paces, but one of the men threw his spear toward the wolf, and the spear landed in the dirt in front of the wolf. The wolf ran forward, jumping on the man who had thrown the spear, knocking him to the ground. The other man tried to spear the animal as it tore into the fallen man's throat, but could only wound it in the side. He pulled out the knife he was carrying, raised it to attack the wolf, but fell to the ground next to the wolf with a spear in his back. Little Star had picked up the spear the first man had thrown toward the wolf, come up behind the second man as he was ready to plunge the knife into the wolf, and protected her protector.

The wolf had fallen on its side with the spear still stuck in its flank and was in a bad way. Little Star bent down to withdraw the spear and saw that there was not much she could do for the animal. The wolf looked up at Little Star's face, seemingly knowing that she had done what she needed to do in order to keep Little Star safe. Little Star had helped her many years before, and now it had returned the favor. The wolf gave a final "wuff" and laid its head down to die. Little Star sat down next to the wolf, cradling its head in her hands and resting it on her lap. She began to sing a sad song about a lover who had died, asking that the "Great One" speed its spirit to the happy hunting grounds. As she sang the last words to the song, the wolf gave out a long, low wail, and died.

Little Star had seen enough of the dark canyon. She gathered up the harness, poles and travois and began her long walk back to Besh ba Gowah. She left the men and the wolf where they had died as she had no digging tools, knowing that the vultures and other animals would pick the carcasses clean before the next daylight. As she left and looked back from the hill above, the vultures were circling the dead bodies already.

Returning to Besh ba Gowah, she was met just outside of the village by Gray Fawn who asked about the wolf. Little Star told her about the encounter with the two men, telling her that the men and the wolf were all dead. The two women entered the village together with Gray Fawn turning toward chief Koko-Who-Travels' and her house while Little Star turned toward the hut which Brown Fox, White Bear, Far Star, and she were occupying. Entering the hut, she went up to Brown Fox and told him about the encounter and the deaths of the two men and the wolf.

When Gray Fawn entered her hut, she decided that the village should be notified about the attack upon Little Star by the two armed guards from the village of Large House. She remembered; 'When Pretty Sky entered Besh ba Gowah, she had said that there were five armed guards that Black Coyote had brought with him at the time he entered the village of Large House. Although Pretty Sky had not seen it, she had said that they had killed the chief who had lived there before, and Black Coyote had become the chief. It was then that the village of Large House had been walled-in with the armed guards stationed at the entrance. Besh ba Gowah would never need that, would it? It had never been attacked, had never gone to war, and had always lived in peace and harmony. But, this encounter should be discussed and everyone should be aware of the dangers. A council must be called at the evening meal this very evening; I will speak with Koko-Who-Travels.'

After the meal had been eaten, chief Koko-Who-Travels rose and told of the attack on Little Star. Then, he asked Little Star to stand and tell the villagers what and where it had happened. She began to tell the story from the time she strapped the harness, poles and travois to the female wolf's back. "I was walking with the wolf toward the dark canyon entrance following the trail that everyone living in Besh ba Gowah knows quite well. As we were approaching the entrance to the dark canyon, the wolf heard, saw, or smelled the men approaching from within the canyon, and alerted me to their presence. I found the bushes behind which the wolf and I hid. Watching as the men exited the dark canyon and recognizing them as two of the armed guards stationed at the entrance to the village of Large House, I feared for my life. They had evidently discovered our presence and began advancing toward us. I cut the straps holding the harness, poles and travois to the wolf's back. They made a clattering sound as they fell to the ground, and the wolf bounded toward the men, trying to protect me. One of the men tossed his spear at the wolf, missing it. The wolf attacked him knocking him to the ground and killed him by ripping out his throat. The other man had speared the wolf in its side and was ready to kill the wolf with his knife, when I picked up the spear that the first man had thrown, and killed the man from behind. The wolf died from its wounds. I left the men and the wolf lying where they had fallen. The vultures and animals are probably stripping the bones by now." After telling the villagers of the details of the attack, Little Star sat down.

Chief Koko-Who-Travels stood and cautioned the villagers to be aware of strangers coming into the village. "We must be aware of dangers in this big new world of ours. Our village is growing, we are very fortunate to have water, good crops, the food sources, and the blessings of the "Great One" surrounding us. I would hope that we don't need to place a wall around our village in order to live in peace and harmony. Do any of you have any thoughts to add?"

Pretty Sky stood up and said, "I am afraid that I have led these evil ones to search for us. However, I want you all to know that Brave Beaver, Long Knife, I, and all of the other people of Large

House who have come to live with you in this wonderful village of Besh ba Gowah, appreciate what you have shared with us. We can never begin to return the caring, the love and understanding you have given us. Thank you!" Then she sat down.

Gray Fawn stood and said, "Pretty Sky, you, Brave Beaver, Long Knife and your entire group of people who lived at Large House have brought much to us as well. We are proud to have you as members of our growing village." The council was over, and everyone went back to their homes.

Arriving at their hut, Brown Fox said to Little Star, "I am very proud of what you did in protecting yourself and our new village. I am quite sure now that I will never be able to resume our traveling trader business. My leg is too damaged to allow me to walk those long distances and carry the packs needed to transport the trading goods and water from village to village. I am sorry that I have let you down. I know that your dream has always been to become a successful trader like your spirit father, Kokopelli. I would not be angry if you would continue on as a traveling trader, taking White Bear, Far Star and the two young wolves with you. I am satisfied to stay at Besh ba Gowah, organizing the building of the new homes, and perhaps helping in other ways."

Little Star replied, "I have no desire to leave you, Brown Fox. You are my mate now, and father of Far Star. Your seed has been fruitful, and we may have more children if the "Great One" should bless us with another. We love and care for Far Star, but we both know that she is not growing the way she should. She has a very difficult time breathing as her little chest cannot take in enough air to keep a bird alive. I am afraid we shall lose her to the path soon."

Brown Fox answered, "But you must think of White Bear as well as Far Star. Is it fair to him that he stay in Besh ba Gowah when there is a whole new world out there that he wants to see and visit? He spends a lot of time with Bright Sun, learning much about the medicines of a shaman, but he is not one to become a shaman, is he? I see him more as a hunter such as Straight Arrow of Besh ba Lakado, his true grandfather. Perhaps it is time for you to return to your home village of Besh ba Lakado, and give White Bear the opportunity of living the life of a hunter, or perhaps even a traveling trader."

Little Star said, "It is not for us to make decisions for White Bear. The "Great One" will provide White Bear with a life that will please both of them, just as he guided us to be mates, traveling traders and now residents of Besh ba Gowah."

Five days later, a traveling trader entered the village of Besh ba Gowah. It was a pleasant surprise for all the members of the village, but particularly chief Koko-Who-Travels, Gray Fawn, Little Star and Brown Fox. It was Kopel, the trader from Irapu, whose father, Peltar, was a friend of Kokopelli, and whom Gray Eagle, Little Star and Brown Fox had met along the trail between Besh ba Lakado and Besh ba Gowah four summers past. They had met on the top of the hill on the other side of the dark canyon before White Bear and Flying Eagle had been born.

Chief Koko-Who-Travels announced an evening meal feast for the night of Kopel's arrival, and then led him to a new, larger house that had been built for visitors to the village.

Brown Fox, Little Star, and White Bear were invited to join the chief, Gray Fawn, Bright Sun, Blue Stone and Kopel, with Kopel and White Bear sitting together. Before the food was distributed to the honored circle by the young girls, Gray Fawn said a prayer to the "Great One" thanking Him for sending Kopel back to Besh ba Gowah. Kopel was asked about his travels and he began telling the stories of where he had been. "After leaving Besh ba Gowah four summers past, I met Gray Eagle, Little Star and Brown Fox on the hill beyond the dark canyon. We spent the night together talking about Kokopelli, Besh ba Gowah, and their home village of Besh ba Lakado. I have not visited there yet, but I do intend to trade there on my way back toward the sundown direction. I have traveled to the area that has the sand hills, where I saw the snakes that travel sideways through the sand. Next, I visited the great waters, where I saw huge fish more than ten men tall, with tails that would hit the water with such force the water would spray in all directions. There were large turtles, and animals that swam on their backs while their young sunned themselves sitting on the female's belly. Walking back from the great waters, I saw brightly colored pink birds that stood on one leg in the water. It appeared as though they were standing on top of the water, but were actually standing in the water of the lake on very long legs. The talking birds were living in the direction of the hot winds, and they would sit on my shoulders as I walked along. Monkeys were everywhere, just as they were when I was a boy in Irapu."

While Kopel was talking, Little Star, Brown Fox and White Bear were listening to each word, visually seeing in their minds what Kopel was describing in words. Little Star remembered Kokopelli describing these same scenes many summers before, but Brown Fox and White Bear had never heard all of these stories and were living the adventures that Kopel was relating. As the sun began to sink, chief Koko-Who-Travels rose and announced that the trading table would be setup the following sunrise and trading would begin when Kopel was ready. All of the villagers rose from where they had been sitting and went to their houses and huts.

Kopel came to Brown Fox and Little Star's hut for more talking. He asked Little Star about Gray Eagle and the delivery of the twin boys. Little Star told him what had happened in both cases, and he expressed his deep sorrow. He could see the reason they had stayed in Besh ba Gowah was Brown Fox's leg. He asked for information on the other villages they had traded with. Brown Fox and Little Star told of the village of Green Stone, the people who lived there, what they had to trade, what they needed, and how Brown Fox had helped the village with the water problem. They told him about the village of Long

River, mentioning that Red Wolf and Yellow Moon had moved back there after leaving Besh ba Gowah, and that it had been Brown Fox's home village before he joined Gray Eagle and Little Star. They gave him general directions to both of those villages, and Kopel promised to visit both of them after leaving Besh ba Gowah. It was getting dark when he left, but Little Star lit a small branch and led him to the house he was given to use, which was not too far away. On the way over there, she asked whether he needed any help in carrying the heavy packs and whether he would consider taking Brown Fox, White Bear and her to the village of Long River with him. Brown Fox would be able to walk until he tired, then have one of the wolves drag him in the travois for short distances. The other wolf would be able to drag Kopel's trading goods in another travois. She said to Kopel, "Think about it and let me know before you make arrangements to leave. We would be able to help you find the villages of which we have told you, and Brown Fox would be able to return to his home village." With that, she left him at his doorway with the small lit branch, and returned to her hut aided by the light of the moon shining through a thin cloud.

The next morning, Brown Fox was up early, walking with the aid of his crutch over to the area where the trading tables had been set up. Kopel was there arranging the displays of the items he was offering for trade. There were the normal jewelry, small pottery items, footwear, woven blankets, seeds, arrow and spear points, but all were primarily small light items which were easily carried on the backs of the traveling traders. The advantage that Brown Fox and Little Star had while they were trading was that the wolves were able to drag heavier and larger items in the travois. Brown Fox asked Kopel, "May I help you with your trading today? I miss the bargaining with the villagers as they pick out the items they want, and I work turning those wants into needs. That is the difference between a good trade and a great trade." Kopel replied, "You have the right idea. Giving the buyer the item that will make them happy is one part of the trade, but getting an equal or better return is our job. Yes, you may help me with my trading today. It would be an honor to have someone who understands the art of trading help me."

As the villagers came to the trading tables looking for items they wanted to trade for, Brown Fox and Kopel were busy turning the wants into needs, and the trades they were taking in were better than Kopel had ever received. The flints were of the highest quality, some of the pelts taken in were finely prepared and washed, the woven rabbit-skin water bags were the best he had ever seen, the eagle feathers were long and narrow. Yes, this trading day was turning out to be his best ever. Brown Fox had become a master trader, even though he was younger than Kopel. Kopel asked Brown Fox, "Where did you learn to trade so well? You have made some very good trades for me today." Brown Fox answered, "I owe a lot to Little Star who has always taught me to work at turning wants into needs, and the trades that were offered became more profitable for us." Kopel asked Brown Fox, "Does Little Star practice the same methods as you?" Brown Fox responded, "Yes, but she does it even better than I do. She makes every trade one in which the buyer and she both walk away happy knowing that each received what they needed."

Trading did not slow down near the end of the day like at other villages. The new houses needed many new things, baskets, pottery bowls, forks, knives and spoons. All sorts of items were needed and the trades brought in larger and more items than Kopel could carry out of the village on his back. He began to think about the words that Little Star had spoken to him the night before. "After Brown Fox tired from walking, he could be carried in a travois dragged by one of the wolves, while the other wolf would drag the trading goods." Little Star, White Bear and I could carry things on our backs. And, they would be able to lead me to the villages where they are well-known and respected. Trading would be much better than what I could do by myself.

This arrangement would help me become a better trader, too. Yes, I will have to think carefully about taking them with me when I leave Besh ba Gowah. As Kopel was gathering up the trading goods and readying the packs to be taken back to the house he was using, Little Star came over to invite him to the evening meal with Brown Fox, White Bear and her. He gladly accepted the invitation and told her that he would be over after stacking the trading goods in the house.

As he made his way over to Brown Fox's hut, he saw Blue Stone hurry out of the hut carrying a small child. Knowing that they had exited the hut to which he was invited, he was curious as to the little child. Brushing his hand across the curtain at the doorway, Little Star held the curtain aside while he entered.

Brown Fox was sitting cross-legged on one side of the hut with White Bear sitting next to him. Brown Fox was showing White Bear a new weave pattern with some reeds that White Bear had brought up from the side of the brook. White Bear was watching intently, seeing every move that Brown Fox was making. Little Star handed Kopel a cup of a sweet-tasting drink that had a blueberry flavor. After taking his first swallow of the drink, he asked Little Star, "I just saw Blue Stone take a small child from this hut. Who is the child, and why is it so small?" Little Star answered, "She is Far Star, a daughter of Brown Fox and mine. She was born very small and has never grown the way children normally grow. We are afraid that she will walk the path soon. In the meantime, we have put her in the care of Blue Stone, the teacher of Bright Sun, the shaman in training." Kopel remembered that Bright Sun had been sitting across from him during the evening feast the night before. He had noticed that Bright Sun seemed to try to establish eye contact with Little Star as they were sitting near one another. It had seemed that Little Star was trying hard to avoid Bright Sun's, gaze, looking to the side during conversations involving the two of them. It was easy to see that Bright Sun was much younger than Little Star, but he appeared to have an air of authority about him that made Little Star look uncomfortable. Kopel wondered, 'Perhaps that was the reason she had talked with me about leaving this village and accompanying me to other villages where Brown Fox and she are well-known. Why is she frightened by this mere boy? What command does he hold over her, or is it just my imagination that makes me think that way?' Kopel asked Little Star, "Has Bright Sun learned a lot from Blue Stone, and do you think he would make a good shaman for Besh ba Gowah?" Little Star replied, "He is a very bright student and learns the important things quickly. His mind is filled with wisdom for such a young age, and he thinks about many things that confuse me. He can look someone in the eyes and see what they are thinking, which makes them uncomfortable. He has done it to me, so I avoid his stare if I can."

Kopel had the answer that he had been seeking. He had seen a similar type of control being used by chief Black Coyote in the village of Large House during his visit there during the previous moon. He had been allowed to enter the walled village by the armed guard who stood at the entrance, but was not allowed to go into the house of the chief. The chief just stood behind an upraised wall on the second floor of his large house, gazing down at him with piercing eyes, trying to take command of the traveling trader's mind. Kopel had been mentally strong enough to stare back up at the chief, and keep the chief from controlling him. It was evident that the village of Large House had fallen on hard times, as he had not seen the fields of beans, corn, squash, yucca and cotton producing the large quantities that he had been told of by other traders who had visited there in the past. There were only two small men and three women he had seen while in the village, and all of them were walking as if in a daze. Yes, he thought, this Bright Sun could be dangerous, not at all what the village of Besh ba Gowah needed from a shaman.

Little Star, Brown Fox and Kopel began discussing the possibility of accompanying and guiding Kopel to other villages. The idea of the wolf helping to transport Brown Fox and the trading goods appealed to Kopel, and he was sure that he could learn a lot from both Little Star and Brown Fox about trading with the villages they would lead him to. This could be a big help in increasing his territory of trade, the amount of trading goods he could transport, and the introductions to the villages they had visited would help him become more widely-known. Brown Fox appeared confused by the attitude of Little Star suggesting the move from the relative safety of Besh ba Gowah back to the uncertainty of the traveling trader route. Since his accident, he had thought that they would stay with the friends they had made here during their stay. Being the director of building houses for the village was a comfortable and important position for him, and he really wanted to stay in Besh ba Gowah. But, Little Star's dream was to travel the world, and he did not want to keep her from realizing that dream. His leg was getting better and stronger, but he would not be able to walk more than a half-day at a time. He really did not want to be dragged inside the travois all day.

A shriek of horror was heard throughout the village as they were talking, and there was a pounding of feet running past the doorway of the hut in which Little Star, Brown Fox and Kopel were speaking. They all rose from their cross-legged sitting position and hurried through the doorway looking in the direction the people had been running toward. They saw Bright Sun, covered with blood, holding the detached head of Far Star in his left hand and a bloody knife in his right. As he walked forward, he was chanting in an unfamiliar language, holding up the head and shaking it violently allowing the blood to flow onto the ground. It was a sight that all those who saw it would never forget. Bright Sun appeared to be oblivious to the grossness of his actions. Blue Stone had emerged from the house in which she and Bright Sun were living, cradling the lifeless, headless body of

Far Star in her arms, crying out in bitter words that she had left the house for just a few moments while the deed had been done.

Brown Fox looked upon the scene and his mind snapped. He ran forward meeting Bright Sun, wrestled the knife from the young man's right hand and plunged it deeply into the chest of Bright Sun, killing him instantly. As Bright Sun sank to the ground, Brown Fox clutched the head of Far Star and held it close to his cheek weeping passionately. The men and women of the village who had witnessed the situation stood in stunned silence, not sure of what they should do. Violence was something that was not within their walk of life and they were powerless to react at that moment. Chief Koko-Who-Travels and Gray Fawn came walking to the place where everyone had gathered in a circle surrounding Brown Fox and Blue Stone who were standing over the body of Bright Sun. Horror showed on both of their faces as they realized that two of their villagers, Bright Sun and Far Star, were both dead. Seeing the knife still clutched in Brown Fox's hand, chief Koko-Who-Travels asked, "What happened here?" Brave Beaver, who had seen Bright Sun emerge from the house in which he and Blue Stone lived, answered, "I was walking from my home toward the brook when I saw Bright Sun come out of his home, carrying the detached head of the little girl in his left hand and the bloody knife in his right. He was chanting in an unfamiliar tongue, his eyes flaring as if he were out of his mind. There were screams of terror, and people came running toward this place, including Brown Fox and Little Star. Brown Fox ran toward Bright Sun, wrestled the knife away, and killed Bright Sun with one thrust of the knife into his chest. As Bright Sun was falling, Brown Fox grabbed the head of his daughter from the hand of Bright Sun and put it to the side of his own head and wept. Seeing the killer of his daughter, Brown Fox took an eye for an eye. I can't say that I would have done any differently if it were my child that had been killed."

Chief Koko-Who-Travels told Brave Beaver and two other men who were in the circle, "Wrap the bodies of Bright Sun and Far Star in woven blankets and take them to the hut nearest to the waterfall trail. There will be an above ground funeral for Far Star, but the body of Bright Sun will be sent over the waterfall this very evening to travel down the wild river, where his spirit will be lost forever. As for Brown Fox, I will think about what should happen to him and decide within the next day. I have spoken!"

As Little Star and Kopel guided a weeping and broken-hearted Brown Fox back toward the hut in which they had been talking, it became evident to all three of them that the best thing that could be done for Brown Fox would be to leave this village. Since violence was an unknown part of the life cycle of these peace-loving and harmony-seeking people, they were unsure of a remedy for this type of action. They would wait for the ceremony to deliver the spirit of Far Star into the hands of the "Great One" before leaving the village. Little Star would go early the next morning to visit chief Koko-Who-Travels and Gray Fawn to tell them of the decision to leave Besh ba Gowah with Kopel the day after the funeral ceremony.

The next morning, Little Star rubbed her hand across the curtain at the doorway of the house of chief Koko-Who-Travels and Gray Fawn, and it was Gray Fawn who held the curtain aside, inviting Little Star to enter. Little Star began to speak with both of them saying, "Brown Fox and I have decided that it would be best if we left Besh ba Gowah so that your decision on his actions might not need to be made. We will leave at sunrise tomorrow, accompanying and guiding Kopel to the village of Green Stone. Brown Fox is well-known and well-thought of there, as he helped to re-route the water supply while we were trading with their residents. Would that relieve you of painful decisions, and would we have your permission to leave?"

Chief Koko-Who-Travels glanced over toward Gray Fawn and said, "Little Star, I believe that that would be a good thing for

Brown Fox and you to do. We, the living, understand what losing a child means to us, but we do not know why Bright Sun did what he did. Both Bright Sun and Brown Fox took precious life from a living person, which is something beyond our understanding. In matters of our own protection, we sometimes need to do things that are not acceptable to everybody. This may have been one of those times for Brown Fox, but certainly not for Bright Sun. Gray Fawn and I accept your choice of leaving and pray that you and Brown Fox find the peace and harmony you both seek."

At midday, a small four-post ceremonial pyre had been erected and the small body of Far Star placed on the blanket spread across the top. As the contents of the pipe were lit, and as shaman Gray Fawn inhaled and exhaled the smoke to the four corners of the earth, her prayers implored, "Spirits of the four sacred directions, witness our grief and guide the spirit of this little girl on her path to the happy hunting grounds." Handing the pipe to her assistant, she received an eagle feather in exchange. Waving the feather from the little girl's feet toward the head, she continued, "Oh "Great One" please accept this young spirit into Your family above." Handing the eagle feather to the assistant, the thin reed that led from the side of the pyre to the inside of the gown Far Star was dressed in was lit to release her spirit to the "Great One." Gray Fawn came over to express her deep sympathy to Brown Fox and Little Star, who were crying as they led White Bear to their hut.

After the people who had come to the funeral pyre had left to return to their houses and work, eagle boy glided down toward the smoking pyre, lifted the spirit from the body of his half-sister and flew up beyond the clouds in the sky. She had been safely delivered to the "Great One."

CHAPTER 9

Early the next morning, just before sunrise, Little Star and Brown Fox loaded the travois with some of the items they had brought with them to Besh ba Gowah. Brown Fox surprised Little Star by bringing out a second harness that he had made in case the original harness broke. Two additional poles had been placed by Brave Beaver behind the hut during the night, so that would allow a second travois to be used with a second wolf pulling it.

After that, Brown Fox and White Bear walked down to the brook to wash while Little Star finished packaging the traveling food that had been given to Kopel and them. As she watched them walk together, Little Star saw the effort that Brown Fox used to stay close to White Bear. He was walking with the aid of the crutch, but he was walking. There were a few items she would not be able to take along, things that had been gathered while living here. But, the most important things were her memories of this village, both good and bad. Those would remain with her no matter where she went. It seemed so long ago, but it had only been two summers past when they reentered this village, which had become Little Star's favorite village. The friendships with chief Koko-Who-Travels, her sister Gray Fawn by way of the spirit of Kokopelli, Pretty Sky, Brave Beaver, and the many other friends she had made over the times she had traded and lived here made it much harder to leave. This was the village at which she had delivered her twin sons, White Bear and Flying Eagle, and had visited the moon and stars for the first time with Brown Fox. She had seen her son, Flying Eagle, eagle boy, here too. She chose to set aside the bad memories. However, the mysteries of what lie ahead on the traveling trader paths spurred her onward, even though the traveling might put Brown Fox in danger. She just had to search for what was around the next turn, beyond the forest of trees she might see ahead, or over the next mountain. There were so many things she had dreamed of seeing when she first started out as a traveling trader with Gray Eagle at her side. She had yet to see the great waters faraway in the sundown direction, pretty colored birds known as parrots, or the monkeys, both to be found in the hot winds direction from where Kopel had come. Yes, then there was Kopel! He was a link to her past, and now a part of her present. Was he also her future?

Kopel arrived at the hut as Brown Fox and White Bear were returning from the brook. Kopel had his packs on his back, water bags strapped around his neck hanging in front of his chest, and was ready to travel. The travois was harnessed to the male wolf, but Brown Fox suggested that the female wolf could be harnessed to a second travois, and Kopel could have the packs he had strapped to his back loaded and transported more easily on that travois. He readily agreed to that suggestion, but did insist on carrying his water bags, as he was unsure of what would happen if the wolf ran off and left him behind.

Brown Fox led the male wolf from the left side, White Bear on the right, with Little Star, Kopel and the female wolf pulling the second travois following behind. They began traveling down the path toward the village of Green Stone. Brown Fox was interested in seeing if his ideas and work had benefitted the village during the past summer. This was also a shorter walk which would test his endurance, and reveal if he could take on the longer walk to his home village of Long River. By midday, Brown Fox was tiring badly. Limping along, he slowed down but kept on going. White Bear had released the birds to fly above the group, and they enjoyed the freedom circling their human friends and the wolves, and one even landed on the back of the male wolf just once. The wolf arched its back and let out a "wuff" when the bird landed, which prompted the bird to go airborne again. A short while later, Brown Fox had to rest, and the birds came down and reentered their wooden cages.

Kopel suggested that he unload the second travois of his packs and carry them on his back while Brown Fox could ride the travois, but Brown Fox would not hear of that disgrace. He was a traveling trader, and besides, the female wolf may not be able to pull such an added weight.

Little Star could see that Brown Fox would not be able to travel any farther that day, and suggested that they make camp at this site. She and Kopel unharnessed the wolves and dropped the two travois in place. The male wolf stretched before taking a walk around the clearing in which they had stopped. Little Star unleashed the three sleeping mats from the first travois, spreading them out on the ground with Brown Fox on one end, then hers, White Bear's, and leaving room for Kopel's on the other end. Kopel took White Bear with him, searching for branches and brush to surround the campsite to protect them from snakes or prowlers. This area of the high desert did have some scattered ocotillo cacti, which was perfect to keep unwanted guests from entering during the dark. White Bear found some small twigs to use for starting a fire to prepare the food they had been given as traveling food by the residents of Besh ba Gowah.

Little Star asked Brown Fox, "Are you feeling better now that we have stopped and rested for a short while? I am hoping that the walking is not too hard on you and your leg. You did well to have come this far, and in another day we will be in Green Stone. That village will be happy to see you again, Brown Fox." Brown Fox answered, "Yes, the short rest does make a difference. It will be good to see our friends in Green Stone again. Chief Brown Bear and shaman Gray Cougar have always meant much to me, and even more so to you. Wasn't it shaman Gray Cougar that told you that you would deliver twin sons?" Little Star agreed and said, "Yes, shaman Gray Cougar did tell me about birthing twins, but he also told me that your seed was within me and that I would birth Far Star. He told me that she would have a very hard and short life, so he was right on all things he told me. Some things cannot be explained but they happen the way the "Great One" decides. It is not for us to say what is right or wrong. It is our duty to praise, honor and serve Him who created us, while doing our best to help ourselves and others survive the many issues that come our way. Is that not so?" Brown Fox admitted she was correct saying, "Yes, you are correct. I know that I did wrong in taking Bright Sun's life, but it hurt me so terribly to see what he had done to our beautiful daughter, Far Star. I hope that the "Great One" and you will forgive me for what I have done to dishonor myself."

Just then, Kopel and White Bear returned after encircling the camp with the cacti barrier and bringing the twigs to Little Star who had taken two flints from her amulet which had hung around her neck. She struck the flints together and a small flame began on one of the twigs, but it was enough to set the larger twigs and branches aglow. Brown Fox, Little Star, White Bear and Kopel sat cross-legged within a small square next to the campfire, with the bird cages between Little Star and White Bear. Little Star turned to Brown Fox and said, "It is time that we train two more birds to fly between the four of us." Then saying to White Bear, "Would you like to have your own bird, and do you think that Kopel might like to have one too?" White Bear replied, "A bird just for me?" Little Star answered, "No, a bird that would be trained by you to fly between you, Brown Fox, Kopel, and me. Kopel will get one too, and that way we will be able to talk to each other without speaking. We can train the birds to fly to the person who is known as a color, red for Brown Fox, green for Kopel, white for you and yellow for me. We will each have the colored blade of grass, thread or reed to attach to the bird's leg, and through training, it will know to whom to fly." Kopel was very impressed by the idea, and said, "That is a wonderful idea that will help us communicate when we cannot see or hear each other."

After eating the sparse meal, the four tired travelers decided to lie down to seek their dream catchers. The moon was in its first quarter, the many stars filling the endless sky, with just two clouds passing overhead, as they looked up from their sleeping mats. There was a howl of a wolf that came from the mountainous area in front and to the right of the trail they were following, but it seemed to linger longer than usual. The male wolf looked up from where it had been resting, forepaws out in front and hind legs sprawled to the sides. It stretched out to full length, got up and trotted out of the circle, carefully stepping over the cactus fence surrounding the camp, and heading up the trail.

Brown Fox was the first to wake just at sunrise, and when he looked for the male wolf, he was surprised to find that it was nowhere in sight. This worried him and he woke Little Star, then Kopel and finally White Bear. Fearing that the wolf had left them and returned to the wild life, he worried about how they would transport the travois and the trading goods that were strapped to it. Little Star said, "Let's give our friend, the wolf, a chance to return to us. After all, it may have gone out to find food for us, or look for a mate. Do you remember the howl of the wolf last night as we were lying down to sleep? I certainly hope that it returns to us, but if it doesn't, we will have to make other arrangements. We will have to harness the travois to the female wolf and divide up the items it may not be able to haul on the travois and carry them ourselves."

Little Star dished out some leaves and berries with a small amount of water for an early morning meal. As they were finishing eating, the male wolf reentered the camp while another wolf stood outside the circle of ocotillo branches, obviously unsure of whether it was welcome to join the male wolf. Brown

Fox exclaimed, "Our wolf has found and brought a mate back to our camp with him. It would be wonderful to have three helpers. Do you think we can train this new wolf to pull a travois?" Little Star went to the side of the male wolf brushing its sides, and the fur on top of its head. Its "wuff" of appreciation seemed to be understood by the second wolf. The new wolf looked toward the male wolf, then looked away up the trail toward the mountain. It did not move, but looked back toward the male wolf. Seeing that the new wolf had not run from them, Little Star decided to harness the travois to the male wolf's shoulders to see if the new wolf would be alarmed and run away. It just stood and watched as the male wolf readied to drag the travois up the trail. Kopel moved very slowly to remove a section of the cactus fence before returning to his packs, placing them on the travois that had been attached to the female wolf. It was time for the four traveling traders, the two wolves, and the two travois to move up the trail toward the village of Green Stone. The new wolf, definitely a female, stood passively as the travelers passed by her, although she allowed plenty of space between them and her. After they had passed, she watched for a few moments and began trotting up to the side of the male wolf and licked the side of its face. Brown Fox had hoped that the female wolf would join the male and left room between himself and the male wolf while leading the group up the trail. After awhile, Little Star took the lead when Brown Fox began to tire. It would take a period of time before they would try to harness the new wolf to a travois, but it was on all of their minds, except for White Bear who saw it as another friend to play with when he would have the opportunity.

It was well past midday when they saw smoke from a fire up ahead, which they recognized as the area of the village of Green Stone. Brown Fox had all he could do to stay close to the group as his leg was beginning to throb and fighting the pain was wasting his strength. When he saw the smoke ahead he was invigorated and knew that he could make the village before nightfall. Seeing that he was falling behind, he asked Little Star to send some men back to carry him into the village, although he kept on struggling ahead. As they approached the village, some of the villagers recognized Little Star and the male wolf dragging the travois. One of the women who was returning from the growing fields called out, "Ho ah traveling traders, friends of the village of Green Stone. It is a happy day when you return to our village. Where is your mate, Brown Fox? He is a hero to our village, and we look forward to his return."

Little Star replied, "Ho ah woman of Green Stone! We are happy to return to your village, but Brown Fox had an accident at the village of Besh ba Gowah, and his leg was badly hurt. He is walking behind us, but will need help from some of your men to assist him into the village. Are there a few men that could help him?" The woman replied, "I will have my mate and his friend come to help the great Brown Fox." She turned to go into the village and came back with two men who hurried down the trail past the travelers, going down to aid Brown Fox.

As the traveling traders entered the village, two people rushed out toward them and were recognized immediately by Little Star. The first was the young chief Brown Bear, while the other was the large, lumbering shaman Gray Cougar. Chief Brown Bear announced in a clear, loud voice, "Ho ah special friends of our village, and welcome to those of you who come in peace and friendship. And where is the master engineer, Brown Fox? He will always be remembered and respected here." Little Star replied, "He was seriously injured at the village of Besh ba Gowah, but has been traveling with us from there. He is being helped by two of your men to enter your village." Turning around and seeing the two men coming up the trail carrying Brown Fox between them, she said, "See, here they come now." Shaman Gray Cougar had gotten to the group by that time, and he was huffing and puffing when he said, "Ho ah, Little Star, White Bear, and I see Brown Fox is approaching. He has been hurt, but appears to be able to enter the village with the aid of two of our men. Your arrival is reason to have a feast tonight, is it not, chief Brown Bear?" The young chief responded by saying, "It is a great honor for our village to greet your return with a feast. And, who is this other traveling trader that travels with you?"

Little Star introduced Kopel by saying, "This is Kopel, a son of the great traveling trader Kokopelli's good friend, Peltar. Kopel travels from the village of Irapu, far to the hot wind direction, and has traveled from the great waters to Besh ba Gowah. He brings many great treasures for trade with the people of Green Stone. Kopel, please meet and greet chief Brown Bear and the shaman Gray Cougar, who has been my friend and advisor the two times I have visited here."

As Brown Fox and his two aides arrived, the group was led to the hut in which the visitors to the village were housed. The new female wolf had entered the village walking next to the male wolf, but looked around at the people who were crowding around them with a very uneasy and wary glance to the left and right. The male wolf and the female wolf which had been pulling the second travois, both seemed happy to have arrived where they would be released from the harnesses. White Bear went over and began patting all three wolves on the top of their heads and their sides, which seemed to calm the new female down. Finally, the group was able to break away and Little Star and Kopel unharnessed the two wolves, allowing the two travois to be lowered to the ground. Brown Fox had been standing between the two men who had helped him into the village, but now he sat down cross-legged next to the front doorway of the hut they were to use. Kopel, Little Star and White Bear began to unload the items from the two travois. There was precious little room left inside the hut, but they did fit it all in with some stacking involved. The sleeping area was much smaller than they were used to, but with White Bear's sleeping pad being placed near the doorway, the other pads were placed in a row across the middle. Since Little Star had always slept between Brown Fox and White Bear, her pad was placed in the middle between Brown Fox and Kopel.

By the time the trading goods were stacked, the bird cages on top, and the sleeping pads laid down, it was time to go to the feast. As they left the hut, the wolves were just trotting out toward the river, and then running upriver together. Brown Fox was led to a place of honor next to the chief in the center of the ceremonial pit, with Little Star and White Bear sitting across from them, shaman Gray Cougar and Kopel on the left side of White Bear, and Red Skies, Brown Bear's mother, and her younger son sat at the right side of chief Brown Bear at the square raised table. Shaman Gray Cougar rose to say the prayer to the "Great One," thanking Him for guiding Brown Fox and these important traders to return to their village. As the food was being eaten, talk turned to the accident that injured Brown Fox, and it was noticed that he was not involved in much of the discussion. Brown Fox kept looking at Little Star, White Bear and Kopel, then at his leg. It seemed as though the torment he suffered while trying to keep up with the group walking from Besh ba Gowah to Green Stone was being relived. Each step he had taken was painful, and the longer he walked the more painful they became. He knew deep inside that he could never make the much longer trip back to his home village of Long River. It would take almost a full moon cycle, and that was before his injury. Brown Fox knew that he could not undertake such a long and painful walk. What could he, what should he do? He watched Little Star and White Bear talking with shaman Gray Cougar and chief Brown Bear. He looked over at Red Skies and saw that she too was not involved with the discussion of his injury. He knew why! It was because she had lost her mate. Her mate was supposed to be sitting where her son, Brown Bear, now sat. He could see that life had taken a turn for Red Skies, just as it had for him. He could not blame anyone for his accident, just as Red Skies could not blame the cougar for killing her mate. She had to live for her other son's sake, just as Brown Fox wanted to live for White Bear. He would be able to guide White Bear in becoming an important part of a village, why not this village? Would he be able to convince Little Star to leave White Bear here with him if Brown Fox decided to remain here in the village of Green Stone? He was convinced that he could no longer take the rigors of walking all day, everyday, and sleeping under the stars night after night. He knew he could travel no further. He was still a young man, but there was no future for a man who could not hunt, nor could he become a gatherer, and his craftsmanship had never been that accomplished. What could he do to earn his way in this village? He could build houses, and that would keep him busy for awhile. He would talk with Little Star about that, and maybe she would stay with him here.

After the meal had been finished, as the residents and guests were leaving to go toward their huts, shaman Gray Cougar came over to the sitting Brown Fox and asked, "Brown Fox, would you have time to visit with me alone? I feel there is something we might discuss together, something of great importance to both of us." Brown Fox looked up quizzically at the kindly giant of a man, and replied, "Shaman Gray Cougar, I would like to talk with you, although I don't know whether it would be of importance to you." He rose with great difficulty and followed the shaman to the shaman's hut. As they sat down facing each other, the shaman looked deeply into the eyes of Brown Fox and said, "My son, you are carrying with you a load that would be best given to the "Great One." Would you like to tell me what is really bothering you? Your leg is badly injured but I fear your mind is the root of your problem. Fear and shame show through your eyes, but there is a request for forgiveness that seems to be pumping through your chest. What is it that bothers you so? Did you do something you are ashamed of? Let it out so that your mind is free to explore a more important part of life, and that is the joy of living."

Brown Fox had never looked at life like that before. It was like a revelation, an offer for a new life, a happy and joyous life. He began to tell his story of what had happened in Besh ba Gowah, starting with the building that had collapsed and going on through his killing of Bright Sun. As there were some slight pauses, the shaman had lit a piece of curled wood that burned slowly offering a flickering light inside the dark hut. As each sliver of the story was told, Brown Fox felt a lightening of the dark thoughts that had been present in his mind. Then he began to tell the shaman about his doubts of returning to the traveling trader work he so loved doing. Again, the shaman spoke, "Brown Fox, you are a master trader. I have seen your mind working as an engineer and as a trader. You have a way about you that could help many people regain their way toward a peaceful and harmonious life. Would you consent to becoming my student and study to be the shaman to this village when I walk the path? Don't answer me now, but think it over. Your ability to build and direct thoughts and lives would be a path that would be important and fulfilling for you. Let me know in a few days if you would like to try this type of life." With that said, Brown Fox knew that he had some serious thinking to do. Slowly he got up, thanked the shaman for the time they had spent together, and limped back to the hut in which Little Star, White Bear and Kopel were waiting for him.

As Brown Fox entered the hut, Little Star noticed the far-away look in his eyes. She could tell that he was not concentrating on her, or anything that surrounded them. She asked him, "Brown Fox, is something wrong? You look as though you are many moons away from us. What did shaman Gray Cougar and you talk about?" Brown Fox did not seem to hear the question as he did not say anything in response. Little Star asked again, "Brown Fox, what are you thinking so hard about?" Kopel became interested in the question and the hoped for answer, and he got up from sitting cross-legged on his sleeping mat and put his hand on the shoulder of Brown Fox, saying, "What is wrong, Brown

Fox? You look so lost." Brown Fox replied, "Shaman Gray Cougar has asked me to stay in the village and become his student to replace him as shaman when he walks the path. He thinks that I could learn the many things a shaman has to know. He thinks that I already possess some of the important traits in becoming a good shaman. He does know that I became violent and killed Bright Sun in Besh ba Gowah, although I was ashamed to tell him. As I told him what had happened, I lost some of the doubt and fear I had been holding within me since that event occurred. I still remember it with sorrow, but I think that he understood my feelings of anger and violence. It was as if I talked with the "Great One" and shaman Gray Cougar suggested that my experiences might help other people understand their darker feelings. He said that I was able to convince people of many things, such as helping them to regain their way toward living a peaceful life of harmony."

White Bear was beginning to understand that Brown Bear might not remain as part of the family if he were to stay here while his mother, Little Star, might leave to join Kopel as a traveling trader again. Would he be taken away from Brown Fox who had become his friend and teacher, or would he stay here with Brown Fox and lose his mother? He looked from one to the other, not knowing if either of them wanted him. It was a terrifying thought that he would be all alone in this big world without a father figure, a friend, or mother. He was almost five summers old now, but that was not the age for him to be on his own. All of these worries rushed through his mind as sat in silence.

Little Star, stunned by Brown Fox's announcement, pondered her next words. What should she say to heal the wounds that were being suffered by Brown Fox? She could say that he would make a very good shaman, or that he should not accept the offer because of the issues that would come up eventually when the story of his temper and killing Bright Sun were told to the rest of the village. Would he be satisfied to stay in the village of Green Stone, where he was well-known and respected, even when the situation at Besh ba Gowah was told to the villagers? Knowing that walking all the way to the village of Long River would not be possible for Brown Fox, what could she say, what should she do? She had no answers at this time.

Kopel dropped his hand from Brown Fox's shoulder, and had nothing to say. To him it was a family matter, one in which he had no say. He asked to be excused and walked out of the doorway of the hut.

It was the cries and tears of White Bear that broke the silence inside the hut, and that is when Brown Fox and Little Star went to his side and tried to comfort him. Just as they all had questions, no one had answers. The darkness of fear was going through all of their minds. What had happened to their happy way of life? When did it change? Was it at the time of the accident while Brown Fox was helping to build the houses? Was it at the time of the vicious attack on their daughter, Far Star, by Bright Sun? Was it at the time of the murder of Bright Sun by a crazed Brown Fox? Or, was it when shaman Gray Cougar asked Brown Fox to become his student to replace him as shaman when Gray Cougar walked the path? What would happen to them if they were not together? Was there an answer to this series of questions that meant so much to all of them? What could each of them do to try to heal the others' hurts?

As the three huddled together in misery, a mysterious dry cloud appeared in front of them. The face of Gray Eagle shone through the cloud and in a hushed tone Little Star and Brown Fox heard, "Little Star, you are my love, and I see that our son, White Bear, is troubled. He will be needed beyond the village of Long River later in his life, so take him there to live with Brown Fox's father Long Bow and mother Little Mouse. He will learn much that he will need to know when he leaves to hunt the huge shaggy animals of the great-plains far to the sunrise direction beyond Long River. Brown Fox, faithful friend, do not be afraid of learning the healing ways of a shaman for this village and yourself. Your footsteps could be followed by many villagers, all in awe of your great wisdom and understanding. Allow Little Star to leave with Kopel, as he will be a good and caring companion for her." With that, the face of Gray Eagle and the cloud disappeared, and stillness returned to the inside of the hut. Sorrow had been lifted, and they all felt at peace. The only one that had not heard the message from Gray Eagle was White Bear, whose head was buried in his hands.

Kopel had remained outside next to the spring that Brown Fox had found under the tree root next to the hill that had formed, causing the water to be rerouted from the fields. He felt guilt having heard and seen the family of Little Star in their troubled state. Kopel looked up toward the black, star-filled sky, and said a short prayer to the "Great One" whom he knew could help his friends. As he was looking above, a shooting star crossed the sky from the sundown to sun-up direction. He heard the voice of his father, Peltar, say "Kopel, follow the star and your dream of being a traveling trader, and take Little Star as your mate after five days traveling from here. Take her and White Bear to the village of Long River where you will deliver White Bear to Brown Fox's father and mother, Long Bow and Little Mouse, to live with them. He will become a man there, and will move on to become a great hunter of the huge, shaggy animals in the sun-up direction." Kopel wanted to speak with his father, Peltar, but the moment was gone. He felt a slight pat on his shoulder, just as his father used to do before leaving their hut. A cool breeze released him from the feeling of confusion that he had been suffering, and he started back toward the hut in which Brown Fox, Little Star and White Bear waited for his return.

As he entered the hut, there was a peaceful and comfortable feeling that mingled between all of them, and they knew that they had been given another chance at good lives. Sleep came more easily than it had since before the incidents in Besh ba Gowah. Happiness was not theirs yet, but at least they would be on their way toward it.

Brown Fox had a dream of trying to travel back to his home village of Long River, but during his dream he kept falling after taking just a few steps, and with each fall the hurting became worse. Finally, that dream passed through his dream catcher, and a lighter, happier dream approached his mind. This dream involved the plans for building houses for the members of this village. He taught some of the men how to dig for the clay beneath the topsoil. The clay could be made into walls. He encouraged others to cut limbs from trees to form support beams for the roofs, and still others to find branches with heavy leaves to be woven into flat roofs. This was a satisfying job for him, but then came the next dream. That dream was becoming the shaman for the village after Gray Cougar had walked the path. People came to him asking questions that always started with the word "Why?." None of the questions had easy answers, but he kept trying to answer as best he could, and found that he had learned some of the answers through experiences of his own. He had asked many of these same questions as he confronted situations that caused him to wonder "Why?." These last two dreams remained in his dream catcher the next sunup, and he thought about them as he, Little Star, White Bear and Kopel ate their early meal. Kopel offered to take White Bear over to the river to wash, and then to the spring for filling the pottery jar with drinking water. This they did, which allowed Little Star and Brown Fox time to speak to each other alone.

Brown Fox began, "Little Star, I know that I can't walk all the way to the village of Long River. My leg just will not allow me to do that. I must stay here and find a way to help this village. I will be happy to help them build new houses. I know that it will be helpful to them. But, to become the shaman's student, I am unsure if I am worthy to do that. I have not lived in peace and harmony. I am sorry that I brought shame upon myself, but even more so that it affected you and White Bear." Little Star replied, "Brown Fox, you have helped many people toward happiness through your building houses and trading. I was angry, no furious, when I saw Bright Sun covered with blood, the blood of our daughter, Far Star. It was something that no parent should ever have to live through. If I had been a man, especially the father, I possibly would have done the same as you, as I had been warned by shaman Gray Cougar, our daughter would not have an easy, nor long life. We were both unprepared for her life to end that way. There is no forgiveness needed from me, as I understood from the beginning the loss of a child. Remember, Flying Eagle was taken from me, and I blamed the "Great One" for having taken him away from me. It took a long time before I understood that the "Great One" gives and takes away. Don't be afraid to face the future as we all should have learned from the past. Do as your heart and mind tell you, whether it be a builder or a shaman."

Just then, Kopel and White Bear walked in with the jar of drinking water and laid it down near the inside of the doorway. Kopel said, "It is time for me to setup the trading tables. The wolves have not returned, so I could use some help. Would you help me carry the trading goods to the tables, Brown Fox?" Brown Fox agreed to help, replying, "That would be good for me to do. My leg feels stronger today after the night's rest." White Bear asked, "May I help too?" Little Star said, "Of course you can, White Bear. All of my men are going off to work while I will clean up the inside of this hut." The trading goods were taken from the hut and moved over to the tables where the setup began. Kopel watched as Brown Fox carefully arranged the less desirable items on the ends with the most precious items near the middle. Heavier items were placed on the ground at both ends, but far enough toward the back that they would not be tripped over by the villagers who would come to trade.

Even before they had finished setting up, the first villagers came to look over the items that were being offered. Excitement shone in the eyes of Brown Fox as he was back in his element. Trading was his passion, he enjoyed the opportunity to offer, accept or reject that trading provided. Kopel sat back on his haunches watching the bargaining that Brown Fox and the villagers used. He was learning things that Brown Fox did to improve the returns on simple trades. White Bear was watching too, but was not interested in becoming involved in trading. After awhile, White Bear left, going to the hut and returning with the two birds, one on each forearm. As he raised his arms, the birds flew off circling the traders crowded around the trading tables. When he raised his arms a second time, they returned to perch back on his forearms. To see a young boy have such mastery over the birds was a surprise to the villagers, and they were very impressed. One of the villagers was heard to say, "How does he do that? He didn't even call to them and they returned to him."

After a short period of time, White Bear took the birds back to the hut only to find shaman Gray Cougar inside talking with Little Star. He heard the shaman say, "Don't worry, Little Star, Brown Fox will be content. He will become a great inspiration to many of our villagers because of his experiences and his ability to direct people through his actions and words. He has a very quick mind, is passionate about people, and does know right from wrong. He is just the person I see being the next shaman after I walk the path. I hope that you will encourage him to become my student." A very hesitant reply by Little Star followed, "I hope that you are correct. He is a good man, normally a gentle man, who loves peace and harmony in his life, and in the lives of others. I will speak to him about what we have discussed, but it will be up to him as to what he will do. I will ask him to speak with you tomorrow." As shaman Gray Cougar left the hut, White Bear walked around from the back of the hut where he had been listening at the front doorway, brushing aside the curtain and entering with the birds still on his forearms. Putting the birds back inside the cages, he asked, "Will Brown Fox be staying in Green Stone? I sure wish he could come with us." Since he had heard that he was to go with Little Star and Kopel to the village of Long River, he was sure that Little Star, Kopel and he would be leaving soon after the trading was done. Since this was not a large village, they would probably leave after sunrise tomorrow, maybe before Brown Fox would speak with the shaman. Little Star answered, "It would please me to see him come with us, but because of his leg, he could not walk the many days it will take to reach Long River. The pain would not be easy for him to bear, even though Long River was his home village. It will be best if he stays here and becomes the shaman when Gray Cougar walks the path."

The trading day was over, and the trading goods were brought back to the hut by Kopel and Brown Fox. White Bear had gone to the river bank, and soon after he arrived there, the wolves came trotting back around the bend in the river, and came up beside him nuzzling him in the back. He turned around and started patting their sides and the tops of their heads. A high-pitched squeal sounded from behind the young boy and the wolves, and as the boy turned he saw a large javelina running toward them. He was not far from the waters edge and had the courage to jump in and wade into the water to chest high. The three wolves were left to fend for themselves and the male wolf was struck in the left side by the lowered horn and began to bleed badly from that wound. The two female wolves had circled to the side and went after the top of the lowered neck of the javelina with their teeth bared. The male wolf was still full of fight, although bleeding badly from the wound. It bit into the face above the horn shredding the eyes and forehead of the javelina. The squealing continued as the animal would not go down at first, but slowly it sank to its knees and finally crumpled down to lie still in the throes of death. The noise had alerted the villagers who lived closest to the river, and they came to see what had happened. It was unusual to see animals fighting so close to the village, and then they saw White Bear standing in the river. They were unsure if the boy was in the river for protection from the wolves or the javelina, but they were afraid to come closer to the wolves. The male wolf looked toward the boy in the water and gave out a soft "wuff," as if to say "all is well." White Bear slowly came out of the water, kneeling down next to the male wolf and brushing the fur next to the wound. By that time, Little Star and Kopel came running down to the river bank. They realized that White Bear was safe, but the male wolf was injured. The javelina was breathing its last breath when they got to the side of White Bear and the male wolf. They tried to encourage the wolf to lie on its good side and expose the wounded side to their gaze.

Little Star saw that there were some lily pads alongside the bank just a short way upriver, and directed Kopel to get some for her. After he returned with a few, she began to use them as a poultice, wrapping them over the wound and using the long stems to tie them in place. The bleeding did not stop immediately, but it did slow down and after a time it did begin to dry under the bandage. The female wolves stood by the downed male passively, not willing to leave its side. It was at that moment that Little Star saw that love between animals was as strong as between humans, and she had misgivings about her leaving Brown Fox here in the village of Green Stone and going with Kopel to Long River. Then she remembered the visit by Gray Eagle the night before. He had told them that she and White Bear should leave with Kopel to go to Long River, and he was a spirit and could not lie. She would have to leave, but now they would have to wait for the male wolf to heal. That would take at least four or five days, but then they would be on their way.

The male wolf took just four days to heal well enough to be able to be harnessed to the second travois that had been packed the night before. Goodbyes were said to chief Brown Bear, shaman Gray Cougar and even Red Skies, the chief's mother. The villagers had stopped by to bring some traveling foods for their use, and Brown Fox and Little Star spent some time alone together before going to their sleeping mats. It was a painful time for both of them as they wished each other well, knowing that they would probably not see each other again until they met in the happy hunting grounds. Little Star told him as they returned to the hut, "Brown Fox, I will always think of you as a protector of our daughter Far Star. You have been a wonderful mate, a gifted trader, and someone I will always respect for your courage and determination. Please remember me as someone who loves you and learned much from you. I know that you will become the best at what you decide to do as you never settled for less than the best." She leaned toward him to kiss and hold him tightly, then they walked to the hut in which they would sleep together for the last time. Tears were in his eyes as they reached the doorway, and he turned quickly away from her, White Bear and Kopel. His heart was breaking, but he must not falter from the plans he had secretly made.

During the middle of the night, Brown Fox rose from his sleeping mat, left the hut, and walked down to the river. Walking into the river he let the current take him downstream until he disappeared beyond where the water spilled into the growing fields. His body was never found.

CHAPTER 10

As the sun rose the next morning, Little Star woke and saw that Brown Fox was not lying next to her. She thought that he may have gone to shaman Gray Cougar's hut, but after checking with him she became alarmed. No indication of his being in the village was found and she knew that his love for her had led to his decision to leave. She knew not where, but she knew that he had gone. It would be of no use to stay and look for him, and she asked shaman Gray Cougar if it would be appropriate for her to leave with White Bear and Kopel. Sorrowfully, he agreed that it would be the correct thing to do. After saying goodbye to those villagers who were in the area, the three left, walking along the river upstream toward the sunrise direction. It would be many days, almost a full moon before they would arrive at the village of Long River. The long walk would take its toll. The male wolf began to bleed from its side again, the two female wolves were harnessed and pulled the two travois, and the poles of the travois broke several times along the way and had to be replaced. No, the trail was not an easy one, but several things happened that helped both Little Star and Kopel realize that their companionship was more than just that.

During the fifth day of travel, Kopel began playing his flute in a way that the sounds were almost like a breeze whistling through a forest of trees. Little Star had not heard the flute played like that since hearing Kokopelli play his flute when she was very young and living in Besh ba Lakado. A number of birds began flying in large circles overhead as they heard the happy sounds. Kopel was happy to have someone with him as he had traveled alone for so many summers. Now he was with a woman whom he had learned to respect, and he had dreamed about her several times since their first meeting on the trail between the Thunder God's mountain and Besh ba Gowah over four summers past. They walked along the river bank, following the flow of water toward the village of Long River. It was a longer route than Brown Fox and Little Star had taken in the past, but this had life-giving water all along the way. The sound of the flute music seemed to lift the spirits of the walking group. The music that Kopel played had the lilt and sounds of a love song that Kopel was feeling deep in his breast for Little Star, and she could feel the attraction building for him as well. She tried hard to think of Brown Fox, their love for each other, but gradually she realized that he was gone from her life, and she was coming under the spell of Kopel. White Bear had taken a liking to Kopel, and began helping each afternoon when they set up their campsite, helping to unharness the wolves from the travois, find twigs for starting the campfire, and finding small branches to drag over to surround the campsite for security.

On the sixth night, Kopel and Little Star were lying next to each other and Kopel whispered to her, "Little Star, I have been thinking about you for many, many lonely nights since I first met you. You were the mate of Gray Eagle and were preparing to birth your babies when I first met you on the trail between Besh ba Gowah and the Thunder God's mountain. I cannot count the times I have held you in my arms during my dream catchers since then, only to wake and find that you were not with me. Now that I have found you again, I will ask you if you would become my mate now that Brown Fox is no longer with you. I realize I have nothing to offer you, as a traveling trader owns nothing but what he carries on his back or in his packs. But, I will try to make your life as pleasurable as I can make it. Will you accept me as your mate?"

Little Star looked over at Kopel, and in the moonlight she saw commitment in his eyes and face. She could see that he really needed her, just as she knew she needed him. She remembered the nights she laid in the arms of Gray Eagle, her first true love, and then with Brown Fox, whose comfort and love kept her happy during their short mating. Now, she was with another man who was more than just a traveling trader. He was the son of Peltar, a close friend of her spirit father, Kokopelli. To her, Kopel was more than a friend; he was a link to her past. Could he be her future as well?

She answered physically and verbally by putting her left arm around his right shoulder, pulling him slightly toward her, while saying, "Kopel, I am happy to be with you, and knowing that the "Great One" does not wish men and women to live apart from each other, I feel honored that you ask me to be your mate. I accept and make a commitment to you that will last until the end of our days." With that, the two lovers began their climb to the moon and stars.

It took more than a full moon to arrive at the village of Long River, but they made it. As they walked up river, the female wolf in harness dragging the lead travois led by Kopel "wuffed" as it saw a few young women washing their garments in the shallows of the river. Seeing the traveling traders approaching, the women shouted out their "Ho ahs" and scrambled out of the water to the riverbank. They had never seen Kopel before, and it had been awhile since they had seen Little Star and White Bear, so they had to ask to whom they were speaking. Hearing the name of Little Star, they remembered she was the sister of their shaman Red Wolf, and that she had been mated with one of their own, Brown Fox. One of the women asked, "But, where is Brown Fox? Weren't you his mate, Little Star? What happened to him?" Little Star answered her by saying, "Brown Fox was seriously injured while building a house for some of the villagers at Besh ba Gowah. A wall collapsed breaking his leg and making it impossible for him to walk. He gave me permission to leave with my son and Kopel, the son of Peltar, a good friend of my spirit father, Kokopelli. Is my brother, Red Wolf, still the shaman for the village of Long River?" The woman who had asked the questions replied, "I am sorry to hear about Brown Fox's accident. He is my mate's brother. As for shaman Red Wolf, he is still the shaman for our village. Let me guide you into our village, and I am sure that your brother will be happy to see you again."

As the three travelers and their woman guide neared the village entrance, some of the residents saw their approach and began to shout their "Ho ah's" to the visitors. They saw the wolves, two of which were dragging the travois, and recognized the visitors to be traveling traders. This was always a great occasion for a village as it meant new ideas and products being introduced to the village, and information about their neighbors. Word of their arrival passed through the village quickly and shaman Red Wolf, followed by his mate, Yellow Moon with Full Moon holding her hand trying to keep up, came walking toward the entrance to the village.

"Ho ah, Little Star and White Bear," said Red Wolf to his sister and nephew. "But, where is Brown Fox, your mate, and who is your companion? Did you lose Brown Fox along the way?" Little Star replied, "Brown Fox had a terrible accident at the village of Besh ba Gowah. He was helping to build a home when a large boulder fell and crushed his leg. He was not able to walk great distances anymore. He vanished after we struggled to take him with us to the village of Green Stone. He might have felt ashamed that he could not accompany us farther, and left to seek his "path." In a dream catcher I had a few nights after arriving at Green Stone, Gray Eagle came to me and told me to leave with White Bear and Kopel, a son of Peltar, a close friend of our father, the great traveling trader, Kokopelli. You remember Kokopelli speaking of him as his friend who lived in Irapu. Kopel has been trading a route similar to the route of Kokopelli for the past six summers, and met you four summers ago in Besh ba Gowa. Kopel has traveled from the great waters to Besh ba Gowah. Now I have joined with him so that I might travel to the great waters too."

The group advanced to the house that was set aside for the use of visitors to the village of Long River. Kopel and White Bear pulled the travois poles from the harnesses, laying them on the ground behind the wolves in front of the door of the hut, and then removed the harnesses from the wolves. As they were doing that, the group around the visitors parted and Long Bow and Little Mouse, the father and mother of Brown Fox walked into the gathering. The "Ho ah's" were exchanged between Little Star and them, with Little Star telling them what had happened to Brown Fox in Besh ba Gowah.

Little Star began, "After leaving Long River, Brown Fox and I traveled to the village of Green Stone, which was suffering much because of a small hill that was growing between the river and the canal leading to the growing fields. Brown Fox discovered an underground spring causing the hill to grow, and during the night, lightning struck the hill and the water was released to flow. The water from the river returned to the canal, and the village was saved. We left Green Stone to trade in Besh ba Gowah. Brown Fox began building new houses there as we waited for our baby to be birthed at that village. However, an accident occurred while he was placing a large boulder into a wall of a house he was building and his leg was crushed. It took many moons for the leg to mend enough for Brown Fox to walk aided by a wooden crutch. The "Great One" honored Brown Fox and me with a daughter we named Far Star. She was born very small and did not grow as other young children grow. She lived less than one summer, and was decapitated by a crazed youth, Bright Sun, a student shaman at the village of Besh ba Gowah. Brown Fox killed him as Bright Sun was holding the severed head of Far Star in one hand and a knife in the other. Brown Fox grabbed the knife from Bright

Sun's hand and plunged it into his heart. Brown Fox suffered much anguish over what he did, and thought that it would be best for all of us to leave Besh ba Gowah and travel to the village of Green Stone. Kopel, a traveling trader friend we had met along the trails we walked many summers before, arrived at Besh ba Gowah just before Far Star was killed, and Brown Fox asked whether we could accompany him to Green Stone when he would leave. Kopel agreed to have us accompany him, but it was very difficult for Brown Fox to walk all that way. We did make it to the village, but Brown Fox disappeared while we were preparing to leave Green Stone." She told them of the dream catcher in which Gray Eagle had told Brown Fox and her to bring White Bear to the village of Long River and ask Long Bow and Little Mouse to teach him to be a hunter like Long Bow, and Gray Eagle's father, Straight Arrow, had been in the village of Besh ba Lakado. Little Star asked, "Would you do that for us please? I know that Brown Fox would be very pleased if you would teach White Bear, whom he considered to be his son, to become the hunter of the buffalo which roam the plains in the sunrise direction."

Horror and dismay had passed over the faces of Long Bow and Little Mouse as they heard about the murder of the granddaughter they had never seen. Their anguish multiplied when Little Star described the violence which their son, Brown Fox, had displayed, and his disappearance was hard to accept. Two terrible pieces of news in just a few brief moments. But then to be asked to raise White Bear as their own? They quietly discussed the request, and its meanings to their future.

Long Bow answered, "It would honor us to help prepare White Bear to become a hunter for our village. It is always good to add another young sharp-eyed resident to our village. He will take the place of our son who left with you four summers ago. We will raise him the same way we raised Brown Fox. You will be proud of him, as we are proud of Brown Fox."

With that, the group of villagers left to go to their everyday work and play while Little Star, Kopel and White Bear unloaded the two travois, stacking the items inside the hut, and standing the poles upright against the back. It was time for the midday meal, and Red Wolf and Yellow Moon brought over a bowl of leaf soup, a slice of turkey breast and some berries for them. After eating, Kopel went to see the area that would be used for trading the following day, while Little Star took White Bear and his belongings up to the cave dwelling in which Long Bow and Little Mouse lived. It was appropriate that they travel up there in advance of Little Star and Kopel leaving after a few days of trading and rest, as it would give White Bear an opportunity to become familiar with his new family and surroundings.

For the first time in her life, Little Star was exhausted by the climb up to the cave dwellings. The climb was not any steeper than the climb to the lookout's home at Besh ba Lakado, but her heart was pounding wildly by the time she arrived there. After brushing the entryway curtain and being allowed entry by Little Mouse, she unloaded the items she had carried up for White Bear. He had brought his own sleeping mat, the toy bear, and a flute Brown Fox and he had made while in Green Stone. Little Star sank down and sat cross-legged gasping for air. She felt light-headed, unable to talk for awhile as she struggled to recover from the climb. Little Mouse and she talked about how Brown Fox and White Bear had been so close, working and playing together, and that White Bear even called Brown Fox "papa." They were both proud of Brown Fox and his apparent caring and feelings toward White Bear. It was apparent that White Bear would be accepted as a valuable member of Long Bow and Little Mouse's family.

Finally, Little Star said, "White Bear, you will be staying with Long Bow and Little Mouse learning to become a great hunter like Long Bow and your grandfather, Straight Arrow at the village of Besh ba Lakado. In a dream catcher before you were born, it was told to me by the spirit of my mother, White

Moon, that you would become a great hunter of the huge, shaggy animals found in the plains to the sunrise direction. They will furnish much meat and warmth to the people with whom you will live during your life. Please learn to hunt safely, be proud of who you are, where you came from, and provide well for your family and friends. I will see you when we return to the village of Long River." Bidding Little Mouse and her son goodbye, she left to return to the village down below.

Although the walk to the village was downhill to the hut that she and Kopel were to share, she arrived out of breath, panting heavily. Kopel, who had returned to the hut after checking the area at which the trading was to take place the next day, was sitting cross-legged in the middle of the hut, playing a game of "touch" with the male wolf. The female wolves were enjoying a romp next to the river where the children were becoming accustomed to seeing them and not being afraid anymore.

Kopel saw the stress that Little Star was suffering, and went out to find her brother, shaman Red Wolf. The two of them hurried back to find Little Star resting and breathing more steadily, but still feeling light-headed. Red Wolf looked into Little Star's eyes and asked her how she felt. She answered, "I feel very tired, and my head seems to be floating away on a very angry river. My chest was pounding hard as I returned from Long Bow and Little Mouse's cave dwelling, but it seems to have quieted when I rested. What is happening to me?" Red Wolf replied, "Little sister, you need to rest. Your long walk from Green Stone has worn you out, both in mind and body. It is time for you to lie down and rest. Find a good dream catcher and we will wake you after sunrise. Rest now, and all will be well."

Little Star did feel comfort in lying down and she entered a very restful sleep. A beautiful familiar melody was playing from somewhere close by. In her dream catcher, she peers out before her but sees nothing. She feels a slight breeze rising from behind her, a soft breeze that whispers to her the melody she remembers when listening to Kokopelli playing his flute. Looking forward, she sees Kopel leaving Long River with the three wolves, but without her. This can't be happening! She sees her brother, shaman Red Wolf and his mate, Yellow Moon, parenting another child, a young boy this time. Then, she sees her son, White Bear as a young man, leaving this village, seeking the huge shaggy buffaloes that he will be known for hunting, far and wide. She sees the buffalo providing meat and heavy furs for blankets, coats, and shields for the many people White Bear will be hunting for, and living with. But, where is she?

The winds began to whisper an answer to her, "Look up, Little Star! See your future!" Looking upward, she sees many of the faces she has known over her lifetime that had traveled the path. There is her mother, White Moon, looking as young as she had when they lived in the Gila village next to the salty river, and there is a young and handsome Gray Eagle, her best friend and first mate. Behind him is Kokopelli, playing the flute and the melody that she had heard when she first felt sleep overtake her. Brown Fox is there too! They are all smiling and beckoning her to come to them. There are other familiar faces behind them, but they are blurred by the bright, glowing light that shines above them. That has to be the "Great One"! And then, from just under the bright light a large eagle flies toward her, and as it draws near, she sees the face of eagle boy, her son, Flying Eagle, coming for her to take her home. She feels her spirit rising from her body to meet eagle boy, and his wings draw her spirit into him. The peace and harmony surround them as they climb higher into the deep blue sky where she knows the happy hunting grounds is waiting. Her path of life is complete. She has found her road of life, peace and harmony.